BETRAYAL

USA TODAY BESTSELLING AUTHOR
TAYA RUNE

Cover Design: Sweet 15 Designs
For information contact :
purplerealmpublishing@gmail.com
ISBN: 978-1-922604-58-3 (ebook)
ISBN : 978-1-922604-59-0 (paperback)
ISBN : 978-1-922604-60-6 (audio)
First Edition: August 2023

Purple Realm Publishing

RIGHT TO RULE SERIES

USA TODAY BESTSELLING AUTHOR
TAYA RUNE

Taya's Steamy Books

<u>**Steamy Contemporary**</u>

Champagne Resolutions

War of Hearts

<u>**Bewitching Twisted Fairytales**</u>

The Charming Thief

<u>**Fantasy Romance**</u>
The Right To Rule Series

Outcast

Lethal

Fatal

Betrayal

Denial
(Coming January 2024)

<u>Paranormal Mystery Romance</u>
Enchanted Underworld
Weapons of the Fae Queen Series

The Warlock's Lair

The Oracle's Court

The Nymph's Realm

The Dragon's Garden
(Coming 2nd November 2023)

Check out her website for all her current works.

tayarune.com

Newsletter

To receive up-to-date information, news and exclusive
offers online please sign up for the
Taya Rune newsletter.

https://www.tayarune.com/subscribe

Content Warning

If you are concerned about content, please check Taya's website for a list of warnings for all of her books. It can be found under the 'Books' tab.

tayarune.com

Trust is earned, respect is given,
and loyalty is demonstrated.
Betrayal of any one of those is to lose all three.
by ZIAD ABDELNOUR

You know what you did.

Prologue

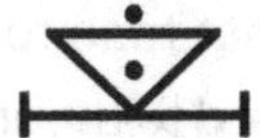

The camp was quiet, too quiet, as if the night waited for the morning to arrive with the same concerned anticipation as the citizens of Segarris. Tomorrow the Right to Rule Challenge would begin, and the fate of the nation of Segarris would be decided. The ominous ancient stone Arena separated the two camps of the contending Princes with many curious citizens, who had made the trek from all over the country, camping in between. The middle class Commoners had taken the east side, while the richer Commoners and Nobles, who had a far more vested interest in the outcome, had bivouacked to the west of the vast round structure. A bird abruptly filled the night with its loud calling, but no other bird answered its song.

The priest raised his head from the tome he had been studying at the sound of the night bird. He stretched his arms over head and realized how long he had been sitting in the same position. He looked over to the younger priest who was studiously writing in a journal. "I am getting nowhere with this," he spoke into the silence of the tent. "I am going for a walk in the hope it clears my head."

The younger man looked up and blinked rapidly in the lantern light as if coming out of a trance. "Do you want me to come with you?"

"No, no, it is a difficult thing we all face tomorrow, and I wish for some quiet time to contemplate with our God." He stood and moved to the small rack that had been assembled at the entry to the tent flap. He unhooked the heavy cloak and swung it around his shoulders, in essence hiding his cassock.

The fresh-faced priest nodded and went back to working, while the older one smiled fondly at his dedication before heading out into the cramped camp. With his dark brown cloak on, the priest was able to blend quickly into the darkness and he moved through the silent tents and out into the surrounding forest. The night engulfed him, and he came to stand beside a tall tree. He leaned against the huge trunk and closed his eyes, taking in several deep breaths and settling his mind. Things had not gone to plan, and he was furious.

He heard the lonely call of the bird again; it was much closer, and he opened his eyes. Walking through the forest was a figure dressed in black, with his head and lower part of his face covered with cloth. The priest remained silent until the man stood before him. "Report," the priest demanded tersely, but kept his voice low as the forest and night carried sound.

"We failed," the black-clad man answered without rancor.

"Tell me something I am not aware of. Clearly you failed or we would not be here. I want to know why I paid to have the princes eliminated and yet they both arrived safe with their Champions?"

The figure remained silent for a few moments before answering. "I cannot know. All assassins we sent died in the attempt."

"I will have to change my plans to compensate for your incompetence." The priest kept his voice cool, hiding the frustration he felt. This underling need never know how much this had impacted the priest's plans. "You owe me two deaths. Are we clear?"

The man bowed deeply. "Yes. We will not fail you again."

"You had better not, or I may have to reconsider our long-term arrangement."

Even in the dark and fully covered, the priest felt the man bristle at the threat. "That will not be necessary."

"That remains to be seen. Tell your master to await word from me. The princes are to be left alone for the moment. We will now ride out this spectacle and see if anything can come from it. I will send word once I reassess how best to move forward after we see which prince becomes king."

"Very well. And please understand my master's deepest regret at this failure and accept his apology. He has informed me to express his desire to make things right and will add the services of our assassins for a third target as compensation."

This eased the priest's ire a little at the bungled assassination attempts. "I accept his apology and the offer of a third death at no further cost to me. It now seems we must let the Gods decide who shall fall today."

"As a man of faith, is that not something you would normally do?" the man questioned.

This made the priest laugh softly. "That would be foolhardy and something I usually avoid at all costs."

"What do you have faith in?"

"Myself and the egos of the nobility." A cloud skidded across the pale light of the moon, plunging the forest into complete darkness for a moment, as if giving its own warning of the times ahead. The priest smiled. He believed in signs when they suited him. He wondered what the Seer would make of it, but she had been gone for so long that she was no longer a concern. Kahlahnni had been the only one that may have stood in his way, and he had been careful to avoid her all those months ago while she was at court.

As the cloud moved on, the moonlight again gave him enough light to find his way back to camp without a torch. The priest gave the assassin a hard glare just to reiterate his final words of the clandestine meeting. "Fail me again and we will no longer hand over the Islands of Lobbregath when the time comes."

Chapter 1

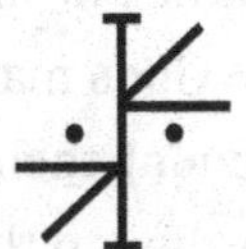

Harlonngraith

Harlonngraith watched his mother carefully, sickened at what he saw as she greeted the newly returned Seer and her husband. "Be welcome. It is good to have you both home."

Evannderth smiled mildly, obviously wary of his queen's reaction. "It is good to be home. I will admit you are a tad friendlier than what I thought you would be."

"We are family now." The queen smiled sweetly at her one-time spy.

Harley had always known how ambitious his mother was; that had been clear to the prince from the moment he understood the word. But as he watched his mother calculate the best way to use his Bonding to her advantage, it brought a bitter taste to his mouth. It was not her news to share—that should have been left to Samarra to tell her parents. Only then did Harlonngraith realize Samarra was no longer in the tent. "Please, excuse me for a moment," he said quietly and ducked out to find his Champion.

The beautiful dark-haired love of his life stood just outside the entrance looking toward the Arena where she would fight to the death for him. His fate rested solely in her hands, and there was no one more capable as far as he was concerned. But the Gods may have other ideas and he wasn't about to discount their whims in any of this, regardless of how, according to the Seer, finely balanced this contest was. Harlonngraith pushed his dark thoughts aside and encircled Samarra in an embrace from behind. He drew her into his chest and she rested her head against it. His heart swelled with the love he felt for this woman and ached for the pain he was causing her and her family by asking for her to step into the Arena today. For a fleeting instant he thought about walking away from it all. A hand touched his elbow, making him jump.

"Put aside your dark thoughts." His new mother-in-law spoke quietly. "They help no one."

Prince Harlonngraith looked down at the Seer. "You can read my thoughts?"

She paused and studied him for a few moments. "No, everything still remains clouded, but now I am home my senses are stronger, and I can feel your bleakness and despair. It is one of my gifts, but a hard burden to carry sometimes. Much like Marra's dreams, I had to learn to block them or they become overwhelming."

Samarra stepped out of his embrace to reach out and grasp her mother's hand. "I am pleased you are here. I am scared," she whispered.

Harlonngraith felt a surge of guilt but kept his thoughts to himself. She didn't need his fears on top of her own.

Kahlahnni reached up with her free hand to stroke her only child's face. "I wish I could tell you that now I am back I have a clearer picture of what will happen, but nothing has changed. Everything still stands balanced. I see too many threads of possible outcomes."

Kahlahnni turned to include Harlonngraith in her gaze while reaching out a hand to grasp his too. "What I can tell you, my sweet Marra, is that I have faith in your father's abilities, and with my urging you have been trained in as many ways as possible for this moment; though, we didn't know what the moment was for most of the time. I believe you are capable of beating any person that walks into that Arena. You are at the peak of your physical abilities and that gives me the hope I need."

"Ah, here you all are," a cool voice spoke from behind Harlonngraith. It was his mother. "I was wondering where you had all run away to. Would you be so kind as to join us in the tent? Brother Arrtem and Sister Innessa have instructions for today."

Without further discussion, all three followed the queen back into the breakfast tent for the royal family of Segarris. The ancient Brother of Wasshu stood frowning, while Sister Innessa appeared oblivious to everything but the flaky pastry she was oohing and ahhing over as she took another bite, causing flakes to settle on her ample chest. Brother Arrtem cleared his throat. "After consultation with my colleague, we have decided to allow the Gods to choose to accept or not the odd Brands on the Champion's wrists. The two Challengers and their Champions are required to walk through an arched tunnel that will determine their worthiness to enter the Arena. If the Brands are not in accordance, then the Gods will not allow you to enter."

Sister Innessa brushed the fallen pastry bits from her cassock. "Each Champion and Challenger may have an escort with them at all times. Prince Harlonngraith will enter the Arena with Lady Samarra first. You will be joined by the two people you elect to stand with you. Once escorted to your assigned area, Prince Tommofey and his Champion will enter the tunnel and if successful, they will be escorted to their assigned section on the opposite side of the Arena viewing area. There will be no mishaps, or chance meetings. Once a Champion falls and the remaining Champion indicates victory a priest and a warrior will be sent out to the fighting area to confirm the death of the fallen Champion. Both Princes will then be escorted out to the battleground where one will be forced to kneel while the victor is given a sword to slay the loser." The matronly middle-aged woman looked around at the assembled group. She seemed so calm delivering such shocking details. "Once you choose to enter the tunnel there will be no chance to forfeit. However, until that moment, either prince can step down from the Right to Rule Challenge without there being repercussions."

Brother Arrtem asked, "Are there any questions?"

Everyone looked to Harlonngraith and he felt his resolve harden. He understood what was at risk and knew this was his moment to step down from the Challenge if he so chose. His eyes swept over his mother and brother, past Arch Deacon Zussya and the two representatives of the Order of Wasshun, onto Kahlahnni and Evannderth, and came to rest on the woman he worshiped, Samarra. Her warm brown eyes looked determined, and she gave him a short nod. "Whatever you decide I will stand behind."

Chapter 2

Tommofey

T he words of the clergy that had visited that morning still weighed heavily on Tommofey's thoughts. He had choices to make. He watched Aviva talking quietly to her brother, while his mother spoke to Captain Albertinne who had returned only moments prior. They were in the prince's personal tent, waiting for word that they could proceed to the Arena and enter the tunnel for the Right to Rule Challenge to begin. Suddenly his mother gasped at whatever the captain had reported. "What is it?" asked the prince.

"The Seer has returned, as well Captain Evannderth. They were seen entering Harlonngraith's camp area a turning ago."

"What do you think it means?" Tom looked from his mother to Albertinne.

"I don't know. It could mean nothing or everything." The captain shrugged.

"I don't like it," Darria added. "Even if it means nothing by them going to Harlonngraith, it shows their preference of ruler."

It took all his strength for Tommofey to not point out that his mother had created that by holding the Seer captive and drugging her for her own uses. The prince was secretly grateful that Kahlahnni had given him a direction on where to find his Champion and that she hadn't held his mother's bad choices against him. "Perhaps she is here because once there is a victor her visions may be required," he pointed out instead.

"Makes sense," Aviva murmured.

Tom nodded his agreement.

"I need a drink," Shai announced, changing the topic. He moved to the small liquor trolley that had been set up and poured himself a shot of one of the clear liquids. Tom frowned and watched with disapproval as Shai downed it in one gulp and went to pour himself another.

"One is for fortitude while the second would be for? Surely, it could not be for courage, as you have been in battle before. Have you not? Are you not a warrior?" Lady Darria challenged Shai. He lowered the bottle and grinned at her.

Before his mother could go off on a tangent, Tommofey changed the topic. "Would all of you please excuse us? I would like to speak to Viv before I decide who will join me during the battle."

A shocked expression crossed his mother's face as she had clearly thought his choice of companion would be a forgone conclusion and be her. "And I am certain it must be time for Shai to put his armor on," he added. Tom looked at his mother, hoping she got the underlying meaning that perhaps she should be with Shai to supervise his drinking.

She nodded once. "Very well. Let us give these two some privacy," Darria announced magnanimously.

Tommofey waited for his mother, Albertinne, and Shai to leave before he sat on the edge of his bed and patted the blanket. "Come sit with me."

Viv gave him a small smile and settled beside him. He took her delicate hand in his and rubbed his thumb across her knuckles. "We have a decision to make." Tommofey leaned over and kissed her forehead, before gently tucking the errant light brown curl that always escaped her head kerchief back behind her ear. "I want you next to me today, but I also want you with your brother, so I will leave the choice up to you."

She groaned. "I knew you were going to do that," Aviva complained. "I want to be with both of you."

"I want to be selfish and demand you sit with me, but I also want Shai to be as relaxed as possible before he fights, and that means you should be with him. Honestly, I think he needs your support more than I do." He kissed the tip of her nose. "And though I hate to admit it, I think it would be best to have my mother beside me during the Challenge. She is the one people remember and know. They will accept me because of their fondness for her."

"Or," Aviva drew out the word, letting go of his hand and climbing onto his lap, straddling him. "We grab Shai and run away. You grow a mustache and your hair long, and I'll cut mine really short, and we can find an out of the way place where you and I can stay in bed all day and dream about a future with no demands and duty." Aviva kissed him. Crushing her lips to his, he could sense her urgency and need to be close. Her tongue sought his and he slowed the kiss, deepening the movements, changing the sense of desperation into intimacy.

Aviva broke the kiss and scooted backward, climbing off his lap. Tommofey scowled at her. "Hey, where do you think you're going?"

Aviva

"I'm not going anywhere." Aviva lifted her skirt enough for him to see her kick off her shoes. She dropped the skirt and looked at him seriously, her emotions a mix of fear and love, but she knew one thing: if this man was going to die today, she wanted something to hold onto him forever. "I want you to put a baby inside me." Her voice was hesitant. "I don't need any recognition of him being a prince and have him being forced to fight to the death against Harlonngraith's children. Your mother need never know..." Her voice trailed off as she struggled to maintain her composure. "I just want a piece of you with me forever." Aviva began to cry, the situation and its consequences completely unnerving her. "I am sorry." She sniffed as she tried to pull the kerchief she had taken from him all those weeks ago from her sleeve.

Tom was off the bed and holding her in moments. "It's okay, it will work out." He tilted her head back to meet his adoring face. "You are my everything, my world.' The prince lowered his head and brushed his lips against hers. "I couldn't think of anything more perfect than you carrying my baby." He kissed her again, gently, before pulling back and resting his forehead against hers. "I know you don't care about my title and would happily marry me if I was truly a cartographer, but I want you to know that I have arranged for you to get your brother's reward for fighting for me even if by some slim chance he loses. Captain Albertinne will see to you being looked after for the remainder of your life."

Aviva blinked at him; she wasn't sure what to say. She opened her mouth to speak but he kissed her to keep her quiet. As he pulled away, his face was the most serious she had ever seen. "I ask one thing of you if I should fail today, and you do carry my child."

"Go on."

"Do not let my mother know. Tell Albertinne where you will be going and run. Never tell her, or she will hound you. Our child will never be free from her machinations. It will fuel her desire for revenge even further I fear."

"I promise if I should be blessed to fall pregnant today, unless you live, your mother will never know." It was easy for her to promise. Viv despised Lady Darria and the way she treated her son as a pawn in her private game of revenge. She just wished she had been able to convince him that going through with the Right to Rule Challenge was idiocy, but Aviva was smart enough to know that her short time with the prince was not enough to override the conditioning he had been subjected to his entire life.

With far more certainty than the first time she did it, Aviva raised her hands and slid off his heavy jacket. Being careful to not let it slide to the floor, she turned and hung it over the chair behind her. Tom gave her a small, sad, lopsided smile as she raised her hands to his first button. By the small smirk he gave her it was clear to Aviva that he was also thinking about the first time she had unbuttoned his shirt while listing the ways she hated him.

"You are brilliant," she whispered as she undid the top button.

"Kind." Viv moved to the second one.

"Beautiful." She reached for the third button.

"Amazing." The fourth was undone.

"Gifted." Fifth one she undid one-handed.

"And," she drew the word out as she trailed her finger down to the final one. "I want you to remember that you are worthy of love, just because you are you," she whispered, her voice hoarse.

"If I hadn't already asked you to marry me, I would again right this moment." He caressed her face before allowing her to tug his shirt from his shoulders.

"Have I ever told you just how much your naked shoulders turn me on?" Her tone had changed as she raised her hand and ran her fingers along them. Aviva smiled up at him, her want for him between her legs growing rapidly, all the pretty words forgotten as her need grew. "Undress," she ordered, taking control of the situation.

Tommofey complied quickly, his sad smile turning into a lustful laugh. "Yes, ma'am."

Aviva was only halfway undressed by the time he was already naked. "Let me help you," he offered, reaching for her.

"No," she ordered. "Sit on the bed and wait."

"You sure do like ordering me around," he commented.

This made her smile fondly at him. "I sure do." With deliberate care, Aviva had taken off all her clothing but the final layer. She now wore only her bloomers and corset. Slowly she inched the silky bloomers over her hips and let them slide to the floor and stepped out of them. Viv left the corset on. She loved this corset. It was navy blue, the prince's personal color, and paneled with lace and satin. It pushed her breasts up and cinched in her waist, adding extra curves to her frame.

Aviva knelt on the ground and crawled toward the bed, where Tom sat waiting, his hand resting on his hard cock. She licked her lips deliberately and flashed her eyes at him as she reached him and settled between his long legs. With more confidence than she had ever had, she grasped his cock in her small hand and ran her tongue over the tip, spreading the dewy pre-cum and causing Tom to hiss with pleasure and lay back on his elbows. He watched her, and she watched him as she trailed her tongue along the underside of his shaft before sucking hard on the tip. Her hand began to pump up and down as she took as much as she could into her mouth, and then released him to repeat it over and over. Listening to him moan in pleasure made her wet and she gave him one last caress with her tongue before Viv let go and stood to straddle him and push him down so Tom was lying on his back.

With a silent prayer to the Gods, Aviva lowered herself onto his beautiful hard cock and moved her hips in a slow, hypnotic motion until he inched deeper and deeper into her. She leaned forward, her hands on either side of his head, as she began to rock against him. Her clit rubbed against his pelvic bone, while he filled her completely with his cock, gliding along her internal sweet spot. The pressure on her core was growing rapidly and she dropped her head to kiss him as she climbed quickly to her orgasm.

As their lips connected, the love she felt for Tommofey became all-consuming and tears began to form unbidden. The increasing pleasure combined with the terror of losing her prince was too powerful, and as Aviva tensed with her climax she began to cry. Beneath her she felt Tom still before he too shuddered with release. He continued to kiss Viv as he pumped his seed into her.

Aviva pulled back from the kiss, completely spent from the emotions of the moment, only to find Tom's handsome hazel eyes watching her, filled with his own unshed tears. "Please let there be a baby," he whispered.

Chapter 3

Samarra

The scene before her was surreal. Samarra remembered the dream of Harlonngraith standing at the top of a steep set of stairs. It seemed like a lifetime ago that she had been foolishly fantasizing about Harley being the hero in a fantasy novel she had been drafting. Now at times, she felt like she was living that fantasy adventure, though it was far scarier than what she created in her imagination. This place was so far away from her native home in Melbourne, Australia, that it sometimes made her heart race to think how different her life was now.

Marra had come to learn she was a Soul Sleeper, one of two people currently living marked with the Brand of the Gifted. Her mother was the only other living person who had the privilege to bear the Brand, and she carried the Gifts of a Seer. At eighteen, Marra had also done the unbelievable and Bonded herself to a Prince of a country not on Earth and had committed to fight for him to the death. It was truly insane if she stopped to think about it.

And now she stood atop the stairs she had dreamed of, standing next to the man she loved, waiting to enter the tunnel that would be their final trial to ascertain their worthiness to begin the battle. Her nerves had settled, and her mind was calm, knowing her parents were here helped a great deal. Samarra felt the weight of her father's sword strapped to her hip, and pulled the black glossy feathered cloak that was her mother's tighter around her.

"Let everyone see where our allegiance lies," Evannderth had proclaimed as he had buckled the belt to hold the sword, before draping his wife's glorious cloak across his daughter's broad shoulders.

"Is that wise?" asked Harley.

"Why would it not be?" her dad had responded.

"Well, if Marra dies, then I die, and you are left unprotected from the machinations of Aviva and Tommofey and have shown clearly where your preference sits."

"If you both die, we will have to travel to Ohanelle and take refuge there. Even Darria would not be bold enough to invade the Pomaikkan settlement for my abilities," Lahnni had assured them.

"It is time!" announced Sister Innessa as she came out of the archway that marked the entrance to the tunnel. "This is your final chance to turn back." She looked over to Marra. "This will be your moment of truth. Your Brands will have been accepted if you step over the threshold unharmed."

Samarra turned to the tall, handsome prince that stood next to her and held out her hand. "Shall we?"

Prince Harlonngraith, first born son to the deceased King Tommofey and current Queen Consort Anzhellika, watched her, his beautiful gray eyes searched hers for something. Marra knew what it was. He needed assurance that what he was asking for was forgivable. He took her hand.

"Remember that you must pass along the message about my dream to Tommofey. It can't be ignored. If I should die, it is the last thing you need to do before you join me in the heavens," she reminded him, her voice, usually soft and gentle, was fierce in its delivery. She needed him to understand that regardless of the outcome the ruler of Segarris needed to know the dream as a warning.

Harley brought her hand up to his lips and kissed it. "I promise that if it comes to it, my half-brother will know what you saw."

Marra nodded once and turned to Sister Innessa, who moved aside to allow them entrance. With her hand gripping her Bonded, Marra counted softly. "One, two, three." And together they stepped over the threshold and into the darkened tunnel.

The Brand on each of her wrists flared bright red for a few seconds before returning to normal. Nothing else happened. Her arms felt perfectly normal.

"Looks like you passed the test," Harley pointed out as they slowly began to walk toward the light at the other end of the tunnel. Two shadowy figures waited for them—her parents. Queen Anzhellika had been most put out when Harlonngraith had elected to have the Seer with him during the battle, while Evannderth would remain on the Arena floor, supporting his daughter.

There was a large thumping sound behind them and both Harley and Marra spun to see the exit from the Arena closing. A large round slab was rolling across its opening. The tunnel became darker. Now the only source of light was the one leading into the Arena. They were about halfway there.

Marra went to start walking again when she felt a tug on her arm. "Wait," whispered Harley. "I want to spend a final moment alone with you."

"Do we have time?" she asked, worried that they may upset someone.

"I don't care. This is too important."

"What's too important?" she asked, now concerned.

"You are too important." He dropped her hand and pulled her into his strong arms. "I can't believe I found you and you agreed to be mine and now it could all be over." He spoke quietly into the stillness.

"If not for this stupid battle we would never have met. I know it's twisted, but I don't regret it. If your brother had not Challenged you and you didn't need a Champion then you would never have come looking for me." Marra told him her truth. "I don't regret a single moment. You turned my world upside down and brought me here, but I know in my core this is what I was born to do."

Slowly Harley lowered his head and kissed her. His touch was gentle, sweet. There was no passion or intimacy, instead pure love. A meeting of souls that recognized each other as kindred spirits.

Marra melted against him, ignoring the pain that flared in her ribs as she pushed against his chest encased with the same light armor that she wore. Reluctantly they pulled apart and stood there staring at each other for a few moments longer. No words were required. Everything that had been needed to be said had been.

"I hope the guy you are about to meet is as arrogant and as much of an ass as I was the first time we sparred," Harley jested, breaking the intense moment.

This made Marra laugh at the memory he had brought back.

"Just don't toy with him the way you did with me."

"Somehow I think whoever I face will be wary enough simply because I stand in the Arena with my father's sword strapped to my side." She paused for a moment and gave him a feral smile. "He would be smart to be wary, but men and their ego can be their downfall."

"Let's hope so in this case."

Harley took hold of Marra's hand once again and they began to walk toward her parents. They couldn't put it off any longer.

The sun grew brighter and they both paused just inside the tunnel to allow their eyes to adjust. "Ready?" asked Marra as she squeezed Harley's hand.

"Ready," he answered, and they both stepped out and into the late morning light. The eruption of cheering almost made Marra duck back into the safety of the tunnel. "Wave and smile," Harley shouted over the deafening din. He raised his hand and smiled broadly, causing the applause to grow louder.

Marra hesitantly did the same, and the crowd whooped in response. It was insane. Kahlahnni stepped up beside her daughter, while Evannderth moved to the side of Harlonngraith. As if perfectly timed, her parents reached up, and with a flourish, removed their hooded cloaks to reveal themselves. A disquieting hush followed as the crowd gasped in awe. It was quickly replaced by a muttering as word spread that the Seer had returned and the assembled citizens of Segarris jumped to their feet to express their enthusiasm at the news.

"It seems your stature and popularity grew while we were away, my love," Evan shouted to his wife.

"I am not sure how I feel about it," she yelled back.

All four of them stood there waving for several moments longer until Harley dropped his hand and turned to Marra. "Thank you for doing this for me and Segarris." He spoke formally over the continued cheering. He bowed deeply and she inclined her head in response.

There was nothing to say; all her words were stuck in her throat. She watched as Prince Harlonngraith bowed to the returned Seer and offered his arm to escort her from the light-colored dirt of the Arena floor. Lahnni turned to Marra and embraced her fiercely. "I am proud of you in every way. Do what your father says, but most of all trust yourself. Your instincts have always been exceptional." She had to yell over the crowd.

"I love you, Mum." Marra kissed her diminutive mother and stepped back. Evan came to stand beside her and they watched Lahnni take the proffered arm of the prince and both turn to follow the guards as they were led to one of the sheltered viewing areas.

"Come, Fiaffia." Her father spoke before she had time to dwell on the retreating backs of her loved ones. He used the nickname he had used when she was a child. "It is time to turn your attention to the coming fight, and I want to check those ribs before we begin."

"Do we have time?" she asked, turning to face him. She seemed to be asking that a lot today.

"Yes, Tom and his Champion still need to enter the tunnel and they won't do that until Harley and your mother are seated. I then suspect the priests will spend a bit of time being pompous and making sure they are seen as important by making proclamations before the battle will commence. After all, once this is done, the balance of power shifts again as the throne re-asserts its full dominance."

"So, that's going to annoy quite a few people I take it?"

"Oh yes. Winning today is only the first step. You have had the dreams; you know what your mother sees. There is something coming."

Marra grimaced, her natural sarcasm asserting itself. "So, no pressure then?"

Tommofey

Tommofey did his best to ignore the cheering and foot stamping that erupted inside the Arena. It got louder and more enthusiastic as it went on. He wondered what was happening. He and Shai stood at the top of the stairs waiting for someone to tell them they could enter the tunnel. There were several guards surrounding them, possibly for protection or to stop them from entering the tunnel without permission.

His Champion belched loudly, and Tom wrinkled his nose as the smell of alcohol drifted by. "How much have you had to drink?" he queried the older warrior.

"Not enough," Shai joked.

Prince Tommofey frowned but let it go. It was far too late to do anything about it now. His life had been hurtling toward this moment since his very first breath. His mother determined to right the perceived wrong doings of the past through her illegitimate son. His time for rebellion had come and gone. His was Tom's fate, for good or ill.

The amount of time it took for the crowd inside the Arena to settle down was unnerving, if he was honest with himself. He wondered with trepidation what sort of reception he would get once he entered the Arena. Would it be an embarrassing pittance compared to the roar that had shaken the loose debris from the stone walls they stood before?

A figure appeared in the entrance way to the tunnel. It was Brother Arrtem. "It is time." He bowed his head and stepped aside.

"Ready?" Tom looked at Shai.

"Too late now to ask me that. Let's go."

Prince Tommofey stood tall, the tunnel high enough for him to stand at his full six foot, seven inches. His broad shoulders took up much of the space, but there was room to walk freely. Shai followed him into the darkened space.

A flare of red light came from behind Tom and he spun to see Shai looking at his wrist. "What was that?" asked the prince.

"Not sure. My Brand glowed for a moment."

"Must have been the testing they were talking about earlier."

"Mmm, must have been," agreed Shai.

Tom turned back to face the figures waiting for them at the other end of the tunnel and turned back to Shai. He reached out his hand and Shai grasped it. "Before it gets crazy out there and we are separated, I want to thank you for being my Champion."

"You are welcome."

"I do understand that what you are doing is for your sister, but I wanted to say thank you from me."

"I did start out doing it just for Viv," admitted Shai. "But now I do it for both of you. You both deserve happiness."

Unexpectedly, a lump formed in Tom's throat and he found it difficult to swallow or speak. He watched as the door leading outside, to the forest of Saffed, rolled closed, sealing their fate.

"It seems the only way out of this now is forward," commented Shai, unhelpfully.

It didn't take them long to reach the end of the tunnel and before he could step out into the light, Shai said sharply, "Halt."

Tom stopped and looked over his shoulder. "Why?"

"Let your eyes adjust. Neither of us want to walk out there blinking rapidly and not see any oncoming danger."

"My guards will be there," Tom assured him. "We are safe."

"Sorry, my prince, but not this time. There will be no personal guards out there. There will be troops of Branded warriors loyal to the crown, not to a brother."

Tommofey hadn't thought about it but it made sense. "Very well. I appreciate the warning."

"Your eyes ready?" asked Shai.

"Yes."

"Then let us get this over with."

Prince Tommofey took a deep breath, straightened his shoulders, and adjusted his long navy cape. He had elected to wear a tailored suit that looked military without it being a uniform. His highly polished black riding boots completed the outfit. He looked at Aviva anxiously standing beside the serene looking cast-off queen and smiled reassuringly as he stepped out into the Arena. A smattering of applause greeted him, and honestly, while his mother frowned at the luke-warm reception, Tom was grateful that no one had booed him.

When he reached Aviva's side, she almost ran into his arms and he felt her tremble as she clung to him. He kissed the top of her head and whispered assurances he didn't feel. As he comforted the woman he planned to marry, he looked around the massive structure and took in the thousands of people who sat waiting for the death of a prince. It made him queasy to not truly know if they were here to support a prince or just here to witness bloodshed.

The round Arena had two tiered sections circling the internal structure. The actual battle area was smaller than expected, with the majority of space taken up with spectator seating. Each tier had warriors carrying bows and arrows walking the perimeter, looking for trouble or unrest.

"Pull yourself together," a female voice hissed behind him. Tom didn't need to turn to look to know it was his mother speaking. "You will be king; you cannot appear weak nor afraid."

Tom gave Viv a final squeeze before letting her go. "Better?" he asked, looking at his mother.

"Much."

He had to admit she looked every inch a queen today, regardless that she no longer carried the title. Lady Darria would always be queen to many of these people and she dressed accordingly.

Tom ignored his mother's glowering look as he reached for Aviva's hands. The crowd cheered louder. They appeared to enjoy his display of affection. "Remember what I told you," he shouted over the noise of the spectators. He brought her hands up to his lips and kissed them. This made a few of the crowd surge to their feet.

Aviva shook her head and smiled slyly. "Forever the show pony. You are enjoying all this attention."

His eyes twinkled at her. "Enjoy might be too strong a word, but it's nice to be looked at fondly for once."

Viv shook one of her hands free from his grasp and lifted it to stroke his face. Several more people jumped to their feet and cheered. "I promise, if it all goes wrong, I will do exactly what you told me."

He noticed several guards approaching and nodded to the one in the lead. Tom turned his focus back to the love of his life. "I love you, Aviva. Never forget it."

"As long as you promise to remember you are more than your upbringing." He noted her eyes flick to where his mother stood.

"You always have to have the last word."

This made her laugh. "Yes, I do. Now leave without saying anything more." Her voice was full of sass and he grinned, completely forgetting everything for a moment. Tom decided that he would do as Viv requested and not utter another word. Instead, he kissed her forehead one final time and let her go.

Chapter 4

Samarra

He's good, Marra thought as she raised her blade to block his overhead swing.

"You're good," Shai grunted, unknowingly echoing her thoughts.

The first few minutes of the battle had been each of them testing the other. Seeing if they could find a weakness. Their styles on the surface were similar, which stood to reason considering their teachers. And while Shai had the edge that only someone who had seen combat had, Marra had been trained by the best Segarris had to offer in several disciplines, rather than just mastering one. Or at least she hoped that was the case. Marra would need to remain clear-minded and employ all her skill to win the throne for her Bonded. But there was more at stake than that...she could not shake the dream she had experienced the night before. Something was coming and the country of Segarris needed her and her odd Gift. And if she didn't make it, she prayed that Harley followed through on his promise and gave his half-brother the note of the description of the dream she had dictated to Harlonngraith last night.

Marra took a strong, deep breath to help her keep focus and it was magnificent. Evannderth had examined her after they had been escorted to their private waiting room where there were refreshments upon a sideboard, a narrow bed, two long benches, and two guards stationed on the door to make certain they went nowhere. Her father had quickly helped her out of the armor she wore and had made her stretch and lift her arm in various ways while he gently prodded the area where her ribs hurt. He had thankfully pronounced that it may have been a crack but that was no longer an issue. She had a minor dislocation and was better off without the tight bandage. He slowly helped her rotate her torso until she felt a soft pop. "That should do it. I could hope for some kinesiology tape to hold it in place, and another few week's rest, but the armor should help stabilize it."

"Thank you, Dad." Marra had straightened and slowly swung her arms in a windmill style. The spot was tender, but no longer did it catch her breath.

"You are welcome." He picked up the light upper torso armor and held it out for her to put on. "You were actually doing more harm by having the binding on. It was restricting your breathing, which can cause a lung infection," he had explained as he redid the straps on the side, and adjusted the shoulder section.

Evannderth had stood back and unexpectedly grinned at her as she pulled on the intricately detailed forearm bracer. Marra caught the smile and asked, "What?"

"Our very own Wonder Woman." His voice was barely above a whisper, though no one in hearing distance would have a clue to what he referenced.

Marra looked down on herself and ran her hand over her torso. She wore greaves on her shins, bracers on her arms, and a beautiful metal sectioned breastplate that covered her from hip to shoulder. All were in a highly polished lightweight metal that looked like silver and the symbol for the warrior was painted across her chest in the pale blue of Harlonngraith's signature color. Her riding boots and tightest black ghi pants finished off the look, and she had her long blonde hair braided in a single ridge on top her head and down her back. She had her father's sword tied to her waist and her favored staff strapped across her back. The staff came to no higher than her ear, so she could reach behind and pull it free, but still swing her sword freely. "I don't feel like Wonder Woman."

"You are a powerful woman, with a great heart, and you stand here for the greater good. You could have walked away at any time, you owe no one here, and yet you fight for a country and its people because you believe it's the right thing. This is not a personal score to settle, or because you feel you owe someone something."

"No." She said the word slowly. "I can't explain it. I love Harlonngraith, I married him at eighteen for God's sake, but that's not why I am here."

Before she could say more, the door to the room swung open and an elderly priest in a robe the color of a moonless sky stood before her. "It is time." He spoke without inflection.

They were evenly matched in height, he only seemed to be a few inches taller than her, and his body frame was strong with defined muscles, but he was no brawler.

After several more swings with the blade and Marra blocking all of them, she began to understand what type of fighter he was. This was a man aware of his abilities, but not impressed by them. He liked to show off and entertain, and he was good enough to do it without appearing arrogant—that was a difficult thing to accomplish. She knew by instinct that his final moves to strike her down would be something flashy and perhaps too complicated, just for show. All Marra needed to do was hang on until that point, and when he took the risk to show off, she would end him. She wasn't interested in displaying all her skills, being the center of attention was something Marra avoided, all she cared about was surviving, keeping Harley alive, and hopefully by doing so, changing what she had dreamed about.

As their swords clashed over and over and the crowd jeered, clapped, and gasped, they fell into a rhythm. Good soldiers did this she knew—her father had drilled it into her. This was the time to expect the unexpected. Marra kept her guard up and allowed him to think he had her. This went on for several minutes before he cleverly flicked his wrist, moving the sword from his right hand to his left and following through with a swing that should had found his blade embedded in her side, as most people would have over extended and exposed themselves. Instead, his blade was met with the metal of her bracer and she twisted her arm for it to slide away from her.

He took a step back and casually tossed the sword back into his right hand. Before she had time to rest, he was moving forward. With his weapon moving fast, he swung it in a fancy arc over and over, and while it looked flashy, giving the crowds a great spectacle, it didn't do a lot other than make Marra step back out of the circling blade. At this point, she almost rolled her eyes and just as quickly realized this could have been her greatest mistake. This man was a genius at making her underestimate him.

The blade stopped whirring and flashed in the sunlight as it swept low. Marra blocked the move and decided it was time to show she could do something other than stop his sword strokes. In a move imitating his, she tossed her sword to her left hand, but while he was focused on that she stepped into his reach and punched him in the face with her right fist. Blood exploded from his nose, and he took a step back. The punch was to do nothing more than hurt him, throw him off balance, and give him pause.

As blood streamed from his nose, he smiled at her in an oddly charming way. "You are spectacular. Who trained you?"

"I am the daughter of Evannderth," she found herself replying.

"If I had known that I may not had agreed to this."

There was no answer to that.

They circled each other, blades joining in a clatter as they showed again and again how evenly matched they were with this weapon. The crowd had grown quiet, and the tension grew. Everyone waited for a mistake to be made.

The Champions continually changed hands, each showing their prowess, every sword stroke countered until he launched a flurry of rapid overhead swings that forced Marra to raise both her hands to hold the handle of her sword to stop the downward force of his blade, and as they connected with a clash of steel, Marra felt her rib twinge, she tried to keep the grimace from her face, but by the look of triumph in her opponent's eyes, she had not succeeded. He now knew her weak spot.

Tommofey

S hai stalked Harley's Champion across the Arena floor. Every now and then they would exchange a flurry of rapid sword strokes before settling into circling each other again. Tom tried to ignore the way his mother held onto his wrist in a propitiatory fashion, showing all those assembled that his display of affection toward the mysterious woman when he entered the Arena should not overshadow his connection with the Lady Darria.

He sat still, no emotion showing on his face, as he had been taught. His eyes continually moved between the Champions in the circular battle ground to the clearly anxious face of Aviva, who stood in a small alcove on the Arena floor, guarded by two men.

With every blow and look of terror on his beloved's face, Tommofey cursed himself for being so weak that he had not stood up to his mother and refused to follow through with this farce. But it was all too late. If he let the fight continue, he and Shai had a hope of living. If he halted the proceedings and abdicated in favor of Harlonngraith, he would have sentenced both he and Shai to death.

The two Champions were amazing to watch. Their skill was like nothing he had witnessed before. Tom's tournament to find his Champion, while entertaining, had not showcased Shai's best skills, which had been brought out by this woman.

Though he loved and adored Aviva, this woman, who was rumored to have Bonded with his half-brother, Prince Harlonngraith, was magnificent as she slashed and parried her way across the fighting ground. Clearly as competent as Shai. But Tom knew something the woman did not know, which gave him a glimmer of hope that Shai would prevail. The great warrior always had something unexpected up his sleeve to give him an advantage to win the fight.

Harlonngraith

The Prince and the Seer sat stoically in their seats watching their beloved Samarra fight for her life. Harlonngraith admired her graceful sword strokes and stopped himself from smiling as he remembered their first encounter and how she had played him perfectly. When Samarra had broken Tommofey's Champion's nose, Harlonngraith had thought she would easily win, but now he hated to admit it, but he was not so certain.

Harlonngraith felt a towering resentment growing towards Darria and her son. His emotions roiled through his gut as he struggled against himself. This shouldn't be happening. His beautiful Bonded should not be out there on the battle ground below, fighting to the death for him to sit upon the throne that was clearly his by birth. He would make a good king, especially with Samarra by his side, helping him lead, with her wonderful sense of compassion and her growing understanding of his need to do right by his people.

He thought about the folded parchment in his pocket, detailing the vivid dream she had had the night before, and the promise he had made that if she died he would make certain that Tommofey received the warnings she had yet to come to understand and to advise him that he needed to seek council from the Pomaikkan in deciphering it all.

Screw them both, he thought to himself as Tommofey's Champion's sword connected with Samarra's bicep, causing a red welt of blood to appear. She didn't even flinch before responding with a combination of sword strokes that ended with her opponent wearing a matching slash on his own upper arm.

The two fighters on the dirt floor before him were clearly equal with their blades and they again proceeded to exchange parries that made the crowd cheer and clap. The whole thing was a revolting spectacle that made Harlonngraith sick. The Gods must be crazy to think this was the best way to determine who should rule.

Harlonngraith watched as Tommofey's champion reversed his sword and drove the pommel of it into Samarra's side for the third time. Did the man know something no one else did? Even from this distance he could make out the dent in the side of her breastplate. Oddly at that moment, he straightened with pride even though Samarra had been taken a beating she continued to stand tall and show her grit. His Bonded was formidable and this far from over.

An audible gasp came from Harlonngraith's side, and he turned to find Kahlahnni reaching for him. "It is done. The path is clearing."

He allowed her to take his hand, wondering what she meant. The Seer grasped it tightly and closed her eyes. Her small hand trembled in his and he watched her visibly pale.

"What do you see?" he asked, almost not wishing to know the answer.

Kahlahnni opened her dark brown eyes and stared at him, her despair clear.

Samarra

The impact of his sword's handle hitting her left side for the third time made her angry. She grunted but gave no other indication that the pain she felt was intense.

"Bet that hurt." He grinned at her as he stepped back out of the way of her blade stroke.

Marra had fought men like this one before. Once they thought they had the upper hand they became cocky. Even Harlonngraith had done it the first time they had fought and she had allowed him to think he was better than her. All it ever did was make Marra more determined to win.

"Why do you fight?" she asked, suddenly curious. If she was going to kill this man, she wanted to know why he was here.

"For my sister."

Marra frowned as their swords met again. That was not the response she was expecting, but it wasn't the time to find out any further information. And honestly, in the end, did it matter? She now knew why he was here; it didn't change the outcome she fought for.

The blood from the shallow wound on her upper arm had made its way down over her bracer and was now covering her wrist and seeping onto her hand, making the grip of her blade slippery—quite probably his intention in the first place. She needed to do something about it fast, before it became a problem. It was time to step this up. It was clear that while the sword was the easiest weapon to kill by, the both of them were too evenly matched at the moment. She needed to inflict some damage like he had been doing to her ribs.

Marra gripped the handle with both hands and moved faster than she had shown him. In a move practiced many times in her parent's backyard, rather than the dojo, so away from prying eyes, she executed the sequence that brought their blade edges together. But instead of pulling away she allowed the blades to slide down, taking a step to her left, causing him to tense his right side, she flicked her wrists to the right, his now weaker side and twisted both hands. She let go of her sword and allowed it to fly out her grasp, taking his sword with it in the momentum. Without stopping, she lifted her left hand across her face and pulled the staff that was strapped to her back, simultaneously wiping her right hand on her pant leg in the hope to remove some of the blood. As she completed her move and stepped back into a readied crouch, both hands now firmly on the staff, she watched him pull a small, curved blade, no longer than half his forearm, from his waistband. He didn't hold it sticking out as many would;

instead he grasped it so it was coming out the back side of his hand, and he held his hand up in front of him like a shield.

She didn't hesitate as she swung the staff. Her ribs hurt and it was painful to breathe, more painful than ever before. Marra also knew her hand would become slippery again at some point as her cut would continue to bleed slowly. This needed to end.

Each step was automatic, as if her training had become one and she no longer reacted or even made the decisions. It was like her body's muscle memory had taken control. All those years of practice with her father came to this moment. Marra shunted the pain away, blanked out the fact she couldn't breathe properly, and stopped caring about anything other than finishing this before she died, because Marra realized with each jagged breath that her rib had probably punctured her lung. *Harley had to live*, was now her repeating thought.

Samarra Kahlahnni Cellecia Durrand gave herself completely up to her training and found peace. With flowing grace and perfect timing, each move flowed into the next. Her blocking and striking, and the twirling of the staff felt natural in her hands, and Marra connected again and again while avoiding his wickedly curved blade. Twice more he nicked her, but both were superficial and she didn't acknowledge either. She concentrated her effort on his hands, hoping that he would think that she wanted to break his fingers or wrists so he would drop the weapon.

Marra inched her way closer to the sword lying on the dirt, but stayed far enough away that he couldn't pick it up first. Now she waited, they were both tired and it was the perfect time for him to try something overly clever to end it and show the assembled citizens how brilliant he was. He was a formidable foe, and she kept her thoughts clear and herself ready for when the moment arrived.

And there it was.

He swept the blade low, spinning in a full circle and forcing her to jump out the way of the vicious knife, causing the crowd to gasp. He expected her to again go for his hands so kept them low and out to his sides as he spun, leaving himself unprotected as he turned to face her, a cheeky smirk on his face. With no hesitation Marra brought the end of the staff down on to his exposed, already broken nose, and crushed it as well as several teeth. He stumbled back and she continued her action, reversing the staff and hammering it into the side of his knee, forcing him to take several more steps backward and to his right, his arms flailing. She followed, this time running the few steps toward him, creating more force as she slammed the staff into the same knee causing it to buckle.

Marra was now in position. Quicker than she thought possible, Marra moved the few steps to her left where her sword lay and scooped it up in her left hand—her right hand still held the staff.

By this time, he had managed to right himself, but his leg was useless, and she knew he couldn't possibly see clearly from his eyes watering from the second blow to the nose. She pressed her advantage, showing no mercy, knowing that he would have done the same. Ignoring the fact she was struggling to breath and each breath she took was shallower, Marra pressed on. She twirled the staff over her head, making it spin faster and faster, before releasing it completely from her grip and launching it toward the feet of her opponent. It got tangled in his feet, just as she had hoped, and because of his injured knee he could do no more than hop to avoid it, giving her the final opening.

The sword bit the side of his neck and Marra silently rejoiced. It was over now, Harlonngraith was safe, she could die, but she had to see him die first, or it was all for naught. Her legs wobbled as the pain from her side engulfed her. Suddenly Marra felt revolted. She didn't know his name. This man, who had fought for his sister, who was worthy of great respect was about to die without her knowing his name.

"I am sorry," Marra spoke, knowing no one would hear her as the crowd were on their feet, wildly celebrating. She removed the sword and Marra watched as he raised his hand to his neck and stumbled forward, landing on his knees before her. His eyes glazed over and his hand fell away from his neck, a fountain of blood sprayed out, covering Marra. She had hit his jugular. She only saw the beginning of him toppling over as the pain in her ribs finally registered as it radiated out into her shoulder and back, making her cough, causing stabbing sharp pains to course through her. It was excruciating. The world turned hazy, the roar of the crowd grew dim, and Marra felt herself fall as she struggled to breathe.

Chapter 5

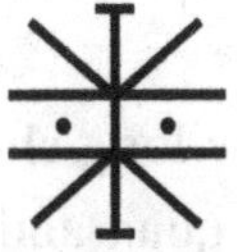

Aviva

Without thought for the consequences, Aviva ran. A scream of horror tore from her throat. She watched as the female Champion said something before removing the sword from the side of her brother's neck. Shai reached up and pressed his hand to the wound, blood pouring over his fingers as he slumped to his knees.

Her brother couldn't die. Viv couldn't lose Shai and Tommofey. She thought she was prepared for whatever outcome, but she was wrong. She had to stop it before it was too late. Aviva was almost to him when she was tackled to the ground, and as she was pulled down, she watched Shai topple over, his hand coming away from his neck as his blood sprayed everywhere. A sob escaped her, and anger burned her insides. Someone would pay for this.

Laying flat on her stomach, Aviva had the pleasure of watching the woman who had fought her brother fall to the ground. Viv attempted to lift her head to watch more but someone held her in place. Probably the person who had tackled her.

A cacophony of sound assaulted her ears as the crowd jeered, screamed, applauded and a chant began to circulate around the arena. **Harlonngraith. Harlonngraith.** Viv closed her eyes against the reality of the moment. Please let them be wrong.

She didn't know how long she had been lying there when the crowd grew quiet and a stern voice ordered, "Let her go."

Viv's eyes flew open.

Harlonngraith

"Y ou need to listen to me," Prince Harlonngraith said urgently as he hurried onto the Arena floor to join Prince Tommofey who was walking from the other direction. Harlonngraith was fretting about Samarra and not knowing if she was alive. At this point, he didn't care about himself, he just knew that he needed to pass on the message to his half-brother as he had promised.

Tommofey gave him a scathing look as he moved closer. Several soldiers stepped between them.

"Why should I listen to you?"

"I need to speak to Tommofey. Move," he barked at the men. He had little time for civility; he had a promise to keep. The two guards moved out of the way. Harlonngraith took a big breath. "You need to listen because this is bigger than you and I. Samarra dreamt something last night and she made me promise to give the description to you in case we lost. Segarris is in danger." Harlonngraith had to shout over the cheering crowd. He found their delight in someone's demise sickening.

The brothers studied each other warily. Harlonngraith began to notice how similar they were in many ways. Tommofey was taller by a few inches, but Harlonngraith was in better shape. They both had strong, hard jawlines, and broad shoulders, but Tommofey's eyes were a light shade of hazel, while Harlonngraith's were gray. Harlonngraith reached into his pocket and pulled out the note and held it out to Tom. "Here."

The four bodyguards that followed the two brothers were quick to stand between the two princes again as Tommofey moved to take the note.

"Step back," ordered Harlonngraith. "He is not going to hurt me."

"But, Your Highness..." one of the guards began.

"Seriously, fall back."

Tommofey took the proffered folded paper. "What do you mean she dreamt it?"

"Lady Samarra is the daughter of the Seer and has the power of what the Pomaikkan's call a Soul Sleeper. She is a dreamer. Samarra dreams in riddles and clues, but once studied they inevitably lead to the truth. If you become King take that to the Settlement, there is a man there who has been helping her, he will help you figure out what the dream she had last night means."

Tommofey frowned and looked down at the note. "Why would you do this?"

"Because she said it is important. The fate of Segarris may rest in that dream."

"Yes, but why give it to me?"

They both turned to look at the three people lying on the ground. Two were bleeding and at least unconscious, the third was pinned down by a soldier. The crowd was beginning to quiet down, their chanting stopped as apprehension grew. With both Champion's down there was no clear winner. "I gave it to you because it's the right thing to do."

"You can go no further until the outcome is decided." Brother Arrtem imposed himself in front of them.

"Fine, but let her go," Tommofey answered.

Harlonngraith watched the woman being held down. "Who is she?"

"My fiance, and my Champion is her brother."

The guards looked hesitant.

"Let her go," ordered Harlonngraith.

"Why do they always listen to you?" Tom turned to him after watching the man instantly release the woman on the ground.

"He says it with authority; you say it with arrogance," interrupted Kahlahnni.

"Perhaps," Tom muttered.

Harlonngraith was surprised to hear Tom agree. "What is your fiance's name?" he found himself asking.

"Aviva."

"And her brother?"

"Shai."

"He fought well."

It took Harlonngraith a moment to understand why he was asking these questions now. He was avoiding thinking about the outcome. His body was screaming at him to run to her side. Screw the guards. He wanted to gather her up in his arms and discover if she was still breathing, but he stood waiting as instructed.

Harlonngraith watched as the pretty woman named Aviva scurried to her brother as soon as she was set free. She attempted to push her way passed the black-robed priest that was inspecting Shai, but was held back by two warriors. The priest straightened and moved to Samarra and Harlonngraith began to feel dizzy. He wanted to sit, to pretend that this day had never happened. How had they got to this point? Brother against brother.

He looked to Tommofey and his heart broke as he saw the fear he was trying to hide so clearly etched on his half-brother's face.

"What is taking so long?" a high-pitched, whiny voice asked from behind him.

Harlonngraith moved his head enough to see that it was his estranged Aunt, Lady Darria. She was one of the main reasons they stood here in this mess.

"If you must be here, be silent," ordered Harlonngraith.

"Who are you to talk to me like that?" she demanded, her tone becoming ear piercing in her haste to assert domination.

"Until we know differently, I am still the one in charge," Harlonngraith reminded her.

The black-robed priest finally stood and made his way to stand before the two Challengers. He bowed deeply, but to neither in particular. "Your Highnesses. I must inform you that Tommofey's Champion succumbed to his neck wound, while Harlonngraith's Champion, though gravely injured, still breathes. Prince Harlonngraith will be the next to sit the throne of Segarris. Prince Tommofey is sentenced to immediate death at the hands of the new king."

"No," wailed Darria.

Harlonngraith was stunned. She had done it. His beautiful Bonded had won him the throne. Samarra had defeated the best the nation of Segarris had to offer. His thoughts were hazy; everything was happening too quickly. A sound began to penetrate his mind—the heart wrenching sounds of Aviva pierced his soul. She clung to her brother, sobbing into his chest. Repeating the word, "No," over and over.

"See to your fiance," Harlonngraith spoke softly to Tommofey. He went to Samarra, who was already having her hand held by her mother while her father hovered protectively over the two of them, but Brother Arrtem continued to stand before them.

"Move," warned Harlonngraith.

"There is still the death of the Challenger to occur," the priest reminded everyone. *Unnecessarily*, Harlonngraith thought.

"Neither my brother, nor I are likely to forget what was at risk."

"I must insist that the final part of this ritual be carried out."

"Not now," warned Harlonngraith.

"Your Highness," the middle-aged priest began.

Harlonngraith brought himself up to his full height and took a menacing step toward the man. "I am going to Samarra, and I would suggest you get out of my way. My patience for this entire spectacle has reached its limit."

Brother Arrtem scowled but stepped out of the way, allowing both men to hurry to their Champions.

Harlonngraith knelt next to Kahlahnni and terror gripped him as he took in Samarra's shallow breathing, how pale she was, and the trickle of blood that ran from the side of her mouth. He went to pick her up but was halted by the Seer's hand on his arm. "Don't," she warned. "Evan believes she has a punctured lung. Move her the wrong way and you could collapse what is keeping her alive."

Tears threatened to spill and he gulped them back. Being king would mean nothing if she was not by his side.

"Can we save her?" His voice was small, scared, and unsure. Barely recognizable as his own.

"Viv, stop!"

Harlonngraith looked over his shoulder in time to see Aviva straighten from picking up the curved blade from her brother's lifeless hand, a look of anguish etched clearly on her face, tears streamed down her cheeks, but her eyes were hard, determined as she stalked toward him. Before anyone had a chance to intercede Aviva was knocked forward. Tommofey had tackled her from behind. They both landed heavily a few feet from where Harlonngraith knelt.

The entire Arena was silent as the two Prince's stared at each other. Harlonngraith saw the pain he felt at this moment clearly reflecting back at him from the face of Tommofey.

Tommofey lay sprawled over the much smaller Aviva and grunted as he slowly rolled off her. He pulled himself up on his knees and growled at her. "You do truly test me sometimes.'

Harlonngraith watched as Tom reached out and shook her. She didn't respond. He nudged her again though harder, before moving to roll her over. The curved blade that Aviva had scooped up only moments prior was now embedded in her chest. She had impaled herself on it when Tommofey had tackled her. Her eyes were vacant and her mouth wide as if caught by surprise. A pool of blood had already begun to form on the ground where she lay.

Prince Tommofey was blank-faced as he looked at his fiance. *He's gone into shock*, thought Harlonngraith. Tom sat on his haunches and moved to take the knife.

"No." Harlonngraith spoke the order without even registering he was going to.

Brother Arrtem again inserted himself into the center of things. "Prince Harlonngraith is correct. You must not touch that weapon. You are to die at his hands, not your own."

Tommofey shook his head. "I planned on offering it to him as my victor."

"No, there has been enough blood shed." Harlonngraith shook his head and slowly stood up. "Two lives have been lost. Two lots of blood spilled to appease those that created this ludicrous Right to Rule Challenge."

Evannderth and Kahlahnni both stood as well. Harlonngraith was certain their presence stopped many people from otherwise objecting.

"You can't just change this on a whim," protested Arrtem, his face growing red like a beet.

"Says who?" asked Harlonngraith.

"I beg your pardon?" The priest looked confused.

"Who says I can't change it on a whim?"

"There is a council you must consider. Advice you must heed."

"I have been considering this scenario since Tommofey issued this damn Challenge. Father made this mess, but I have no desire to carry it on and cause a greater divide in our nation. My brother will not die by my hand today. I am King and this is my decree."

"There has been no coronation," Arrtem attempted to explain.

"You and I both know that is a mere formality. This farce today made me king. And my first official order as King of Segarris is to abolish this ridiculous Right to Rule law."

Tommofey stood and blinked at Harlonngraith. "Are you sure?"

"I will have to ratify the decision once I am crowned and I am certain others will try to dissuade me, but yes, this is done. Find peace if you can."

Prince Tommofey, third born son of King Tommofey, once King of Segarris, dropped to one knee, and the crowd that had been silent went wild. Tom held out his hand and Harlonngraith took it. Tom rested his forehead on the back of Harlonngraith's hand for several seconds, clearly pledging his allegiance to the new king. He then let go and stood once more.

Loudly, to be heard over the cheering Tom said, "Aviva was right. I am too selfish to be king. All I thought about was winning and stopping my mother from telling me what to do, and you have been considering how to forgive and move forward and change the law to stop this stupidity." And with that, Tommofey bent down and gently picked up the body of Aviva before instructing another soldier to carry Shai. And with a little procession of guards, the prince carried his fiance into the small chamber they had originally been assigned to earlier that morning.

Harlonngraith shook his head and turned back to face his bleak future of being a king with no queen.

"I don't think there is anything we can do for her now, except make her comfortable." Kahlahnni spoke softly, her grief palpable to Harlonngraith as she looked down at her only daughter.

Harlonngraith could only nod. He was beyond understanding anything further as wave after wave of heartache came over him at the thought of losing Samarra.

Evannderth grasped his shoulder. "Grief must wait. You are king and you just showed everyone you are willing to make hard but fair decisions. You must continue this now."

"What would you have me do?" Harlonngraith bit back the harsh words he wanted to utter, focusing on reminding himself that Evannderth, like Kahlahnni, were facing the death of their daughter with far more stoic grace than he was.

"Stand, wave to the crowd, and order the guards to start moving the people out. Have someone watch over Tommofey and Darria to make certain they do nothing silly as they return to their camp. Once we are alone, we will then keep vigil as our brave girl takes her final breaths." Evannderth's voice broke on his final words.

Chapter 6

Samarra

The sound of beeping infiltrated her dream and Marra struggled to wake. A cool hand touched her forehead and what she recognized as her father's voice spoke softly. "Faffia, you are home and safe. You had a motorbike accident on the property."

Marra tried to shake her head. She was confused. What was he talking about? She had never even ridden a motorbike. The sound of cars registered in her head, to join the beeping of the machines, and it all fell into place. She was not in Segarris, somehow she was back in Melbourne, Australia, and by the sound of the machine and the smell around her, she was in a hospital bed. Her eyes fluttered open to discover she was in a single bedroom, the curtain drawn against a darkened sky, her father hovered over her, a huge grin on his face.

"Why are you smiling like a maniac?" She frowned at him, her voice croaky and her throat dry.

"You are alive." Tears spilled from his aquamarine eyes. "And I am grateful to all the Gods."

Marra was taken back to the moment she watched her opponent collapse and die, knowing that the pain and difficulty she was having breathing and the taste of blood in her mouth she would more than likely join him quickly.

"How?" she asked.

Before her father could answer, a nurse hurried into the room and smiled warmly.

"Ah, it is nice to see you awake. No sudden moves, okay? You took quite the tumble from your bike. Several broken ribs, a fully collapsed lung, a bruised spleen, and many gashes where you went through the greenhouse window. I don't think riding bikes is for you, or next time do it with protective gear on." He raised an eyebrow at her before turning to check her IV machine. "I bet you're hungry?" The nurse turned back to Marra, an expectant look on his chubby face.

She nodded.

"It's late, so they have stopped serving dinner, but we always keep sandwiches in the fridge for these moments. Will that do?"

"Yes, please."

He nodded and gave her another smile. "Perhaps you can persuade your father to leave now you are awake. He needs to shower and change." The middle-aged nurse gave Evannderth a friendly side-eyed glance and wrinkled his nose to imply he smelled. "I'll be back shortly with food. Anything else you need?"

"No, thank you."

The nurse hurried from the room and Marra turned back to Evan. "Dad, what happened? Is Harley alright? I was certain I was about to die," she whispered.

He reached out and took her hand, giving it a gentle squeeze. "You won, my beautiful brave girl. I am proud of you." He pulled his chair closer and sat down, still gripping her hand. "You were right. Your mother and I knew you were dying the moment we got to you." His voice was soft, barely audible over the intrusive noises of the modern world. "Harlonngraith ordered everyone out of the Arena, and I mean everyone. Your mother insisted. She said it was important but didn't know why. We both knew better than to argue."

Marra nodded her head. "Yes, if Mum insists then you listen, especially now I understand how special she is."

"The three of us sat on the dirt, watching you struggle to breath and feeling hopeless. I told your mother and Bonded about the rib damage you sustained during the assassination attempt and we all agreed to not move you, as we had all witnessed Shai hitting that weak spot several times during the battle."

"His name was Shai?" she asked, her throat constricted at the word.

"Yes."

"We were so evenly matched."

"Yes, you both were exceptional."

"Dad..." A sob escaped her and she tried to keep control of her emotions but a wave of guilt and relief overcame her. "I killed him," she whispered. "I picked up your sword and with clear calculation buried it into the side of his neck."

"Faffia, you made a choice. We make choices everyday, some minor and insignificant, most major ones only affect those closest to us, and on rare occasions our choices are crucial to a nation. You chose to fight for Segarris and Harlonngraith, the rightful heir, a good, kind young man whose first decision as king was to denounce the Right to Rule Challenge and allow Tommofey to live. And Shai, like you, made the choice to fight. He chose to weaken, not understand you as an opponent. That was his fatal flaw. Your skill levels were mostly on par, though you have more range, it was the ability to read the nuance of his opponent that was lacking, but that is the way of a soldier. He found your physical weakness and honed in on it as he was a fraction physically stronger. You found his mental weakness and that is how you won."

She sniffed and nodded, taking in his words. "He was fighting for his sister." Marra didn't know why she needed her father to understand Shai's motivations.

"A reason no less honorable than yours. Family is everything."

Marra smiled weakly. "How did I survive? Even by the fastest route of rivers and carriages the Arena is weeks away from the portal and by your own admission moving me would be fatal."

"Do you remember a black-robed priest?"

Marra frowned. "I don't think so."

"The elderly priest who came to escort you to the Arena after I had looked at your ribs?"

"Mmmm, vaguely."

"He approached us while we prayed for you and told us that he may be able to help with your healing if we trusted him to do something unusual, but we were not to ask questions.

"By this point all three of us had come to the conclusion you were mere moments away from leaving us. Your breathing was now full of a rattle and so shallow. Harlonngraith agreed immediately and we were told to stand and face away from you. I have no idea what the priest did, but no more than ten minutes later he told us we could turn back. We found that your face had changed. Your lines had smoothed, and your mouth gone slack, you no longer looked in pain. At first we thought he had killed you, but then he had explained he had put you in some kind of stasis, I guess like an induced coma, but we couldn't harm you if we moved you, as long as we kept you flat you would remain safe from your wounds and doing any further damage. At that point, we didn't care how he had done it, we were just grateful and wanted to know how long it would last. He told us that if he traveled with us he could keep you like that for several months, but that you would waste away and eventually die."

Evannderth stopped and took in a breath, before continuing. "It was touch and go for a while there. Harlonngraith sent men ahead to prepare and clear the way. He organized carts, carriages, boats, and anything else to make our travel expedient. Everyone thought we were trying to get you back to the capital to the best doctors, but we knew they couldn't save you. Only modern medicine would be able to heal you by this point. The people of Segarris believe you to be recuperating in the palace. Under the cover of darkness, we entered the palace and sent a decoy up to your rooms while the four of us, with Arch Deacon Zussya, headed to the portal. We dressed you in the clothes you came through in and I carried you through, pretending you had fainted in the bookstore. I called an ambulance and told them you had passed out. That you had had a motorbike crash that morning but had assured me you were fine."

"How long have I been here?"

"I brought you through four days ago. They kept you under light sedation for the past few days after you had surgery to re-inflate the lung and heal the puncture, just to stop you from moving. Your dreams have been pretty intense, and it was the only way to get you to settle."

The nurse entered the room with a covered tray. "Here we go. Managed to find you some sandwiches, custard, and juice."

Marra smiled gratefully. "Thank you." She was propped up on several pillows but looked around to find the remote to raise her higher.

"It's right by your side, but don't twist to get it," the nurse told her.

"Here, Faffia." Evan held it up.

"Thanks, Dad." Marra took it from him and studied the remote to figure out which button to press. After finding a comfortable position she looked up at the nurse. "When can I go home?"

"That's something you can discuss with your doctor when he comes in for his rounds in the morning." A buzzer sounded in the quiet hallway. "I am being summoned. Press the button if you need me for anything. I'll be back in to check your vitals soon."

Marra unwrapped her sandwiches that were cut into four triangles and offered her father one. He shook his head.

"You look awful. How much sleep are you getting?" she asked.

"I am getting snippets of sleep. I think the painkillers they were giving you were making you more open to your dreams, so I have been singing to you on and off for several days. They have started to wean you off the hard stuff now, which should help your mental barriers snap back in, and combined with Earth's natural interference keep the dreams down, especially now that you have been trained by the Pomaikka."

"It would be nice to sleep without bothering others for once."

"You have never been a bother."

"Doesn't feel like it but thank you for saying it."

They ate the food in silence, the only sounds were the beeping of the machines and the occasional car on the street outside. Marra finished her custard and settled back on her pillow, lowering the top half of the bed a little. She carefully tested taking a deeper breath and was met by a dull pain rather than a sharp one. She began to cough and winced.

"How's the pain level?" the nurse asked as he came in.

"Not too bad." Marra took a sip of water.

"Not too bad, I *crashed my bike through a greenhouse window and pretended I was fine until my lung collapsed* pain, or it's not too bad *and I am surprised it doesn't hurt more* pain?"

She laughed shyly. "The *I am surprised it doesn't hurt more* type."

"Okay, let's get you something not too heavy and see how you go. You just have to promise me that if the pain worsens you will not be a hero and admit it."

"I promise."

"Good." The nurse turned to Evan. "And now you know she is fine, it is time for you to go home and rest. For at least a few hours. She needs fresh clothes and toiletries, and you need to take a break."

Evan nodded. "I will go once she is asleep."

The nurse stared at Evan for a few moments longer. "I can see you love your daughter very much, but I promise nothing will happen to her while you are gone."

"I will go when she has had her pain killers and is asleep," Evan said firmly.

"Dad, it's okay. I don't think I can sleep for a while. I feel like I have been asleep for weeks." Marra winked at him, hoping he got the joke.

He smirked at her comment and she watched him relax. She squeezed his hand. "I know you have been worried, but seriously I am good. Go and get some rest. Just bring me what you think I'll need."

The nurse interrupted them. "You can always text him a list of what you need."

Marra blinked at him for several moments before what he said made sense. She had forgotten where she was. "I don't have my phone with me," she explained. "I am trying to detox from it."

"Wish I could," he lamented. "I deleted my social media and three days later I am suffering serious FOMO."

This made her laugh. The thought of having her phone and checking in with her girlfriends was appealing. It was definitely something she had missed. "My phone and laptop would be great. I'll do some work for the dojo while I am here."

Her father looked at her, a strange expression on his face, and Marra wondered what she had said to bring it on.

Chapter 7

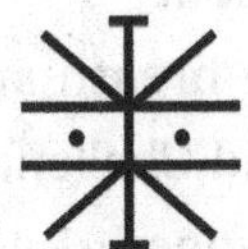

Harlonngraith

"Honestly, what were you thinking?" she fumed at him as she tossed the parchment on his desk.

"Mother, you have already said your peace. Must we do this again?" Harlonngraith kept his voice even though he knew there was an edge creeping in. He found his mother exhausting.

"You should have had them both killed. Now she offers insult by declining the invitation to your coronation."

Harlonngraith picked up the discarded paper and scanned its content. It was a short hand-written note expressing regret that Lady Darria, former Queen of Segarris, would be unable to attend the upcoming coronation.

"She should be forced to come and watch, and so should her son," Queen Anzhellika continued on her tirade.

"Nowhere in that note does it say Tommofey will not be attending." He tried to reason with her.

"I can't believe any son of mine would be foolish enough to allow this farce to happen. You would never have done this before you met—"

Harlonngraith cut her off before she could go any further. "Don't say it."

Her icy blue eyes widened at his tone. "Do not think you command me, my son."

He took a steadying breath and kept his temper. "I never wanted the stupid Challenge, and I never had any intention of killing anyone if I could possibly help it. I prayed all along that Tommofey would back out. This fighting between the family needs to stop. The Seer has been warning our family for years that something is coming, and Samarra dreamed of a huge fleet of ships bearing down on us, we do not have time for tantrums and such." Harlonngraith emphasized his new authority by sitting behind the desk that had been his father's, that Anzhellika had been using as her own up until two weeks ago.

"You know nothing about Tommofey. He could be plotting your death for all we know," she persisted.

"Mother, I am not a fool. You had me trained by the best. I am not blindly trusting him, nor anyone else."

"I have sacrificed much to gain us the throne. I will not have it jeopardized by your newly found morals."

Harlonngraith surged to his feet and glowered at the tall blonde woman on the other side of the ornate desk. "What are you talking about? Do you think for one moment if the Seer didn't think I was a good person she would have allowed her daughter to enter the Arena for me? Do you think Evannderth would have? What about the Pomaikkan or the Gods that allow her to wear the Gifted Brand? You insult me and your intelligence with this ludicrous conversation. If I didn't know better, I would think you are not yet ready to hand over your power or sway over me." He spoke with a deceptive calmness, while inside he was shocked at his mother's blatant lust for power. How had he not seen it before?

Anzhellika was the first to break eye contact. She settled into the winged back chair, with its rich velvet cover in the palest blue, taking several moments to adjust her full skirts around her legs. Her voice was calm when she finally spoke. "I asked for none of this. It is not my fault my sister could not conceive, and your father cast her aside and chose me, and I was easily able to have both you and your brother. I did not ask for him to betray me by running back to Darria and having that bastard Tommofey. I certainly did not ask for him to die without naming you as heir which then opened the way for the Challenge to be issued. How can you accuse me of coveting power when all I have done is react to the situations I have found myself in?"

In just a few steps, Harlonngraith walked around the desk and sat next to his mother on the second blue covered chair. He held out his hand and she took it. "I am sorry. I do not mean to fight with you."

"My beautiful boy, all I have ever wanted for you is what you are rightfully entitled to. Nothing more, nothing less." She patted his hand. "You will make an excellent king, if you just remember that not everyone deserves forgiveness."

"I am worried," Harlonngraith admitted.

"There is nothing to be concerned about. As you said before, you have learned your lessons well and with the

right guidance all will be well," Anzhellika spoke sooth-
ingly.

Harlonngraith shook his head. "No, that's not what I
meant." It saddened him to recognize that all his mother
thought about was him being king. Could she not see how
upset he was? "I am worried about Samarra. There has
been no word of her condition."

"Send word to the priest that cares for her and demand
to know what is happening."

The room grew silent as he thought about his mother's
words. If only it was that easy. His Bonded was not anywhere he could send word to. She had been carried by
Evannderth through the portal several weeks ago, while
Kahlahnni had stayed behind keeping up the pretense
that Samarra was still in the city. At night, when Harlonngraith was alone, all he could do was think of his strong,
beautiful warrior who had fought for him and that she
could be dying in a hospital bed in Melbourne and he
would never know. He tried not to think about what he
would do if Evannderth came through and told him that
she lived, but that Samarra was choosing not to return,
that her home was on Earth and that she had sacrificed
enough for him. He had his throne now. Would he give it
all up for the woman he loved? The longer he didn't know
what was happening and the more his mother demanded
he rule her way, the more appealing the idea of giving it
all up and stepping through the portal forever became to
him.

Harlonngraith shook off his dark thoughts; they didn't
help him now. He needed to remain focused on the cur-

rent concerns and the upcoming coronation. A thought suddenly occurred to him and he let go of his mother's hand and stood to walk back around the desk, tugging on one of the bell pulls that sat behind his desk. A few moments later the door to his private study opened and his private steward stood there. "How may I serve you?"

"Find me the Seer. I wish to discuss something with her at her earliest convenience."

"Very well, Your Majesty."

"Why do you wish to speak to her?" Anzhellika asked.

"Near the end of the Challenge, Kahlahnni told me that her vision had cleared. There were so many other things going on that it didn't really sink in until now. I want to know what she meant by it."

Chapter 8

Samarra

Marra waved goodbye to the car as it drove around the bend of her driveway and out of sight. She had thought catching up with her friends would be a wonderful idea, but in the end, she had had to tell so many lies it became exhausting trying to keep it all straight, and she felt guilty.

It was a warm Melbourne afternoon and Marra was thinking she might grab a book and sit out on the patio to read for a while. She needed to keep her mind active or she was going to go stir crazy. Not being able to exercise other than a light walk was making her feel restless and useless. Reading might help alleviate the constant worry and ache in her heart too. She poured herself a second glass of fruit punch and carried it out to the table, before heading back into the house to find something that might hold her attention.

The last three weeks had dragged since being discharged from the hospital. Another three days and she would get the stitches on her ribs and upper arm checked and hopefully removed, and then fingers crossed, given the clear to slowly get back into training. She looked forward to visiting the dojo and checking in on the children.

Choosing a book she had comfort read so often the edges were worn and the cover faded, Marra headed back out to the padded lounge chair on the patio.

"Come and sit with me," Evan called from the entrance to the family's personal glade. He was tugging gardening gloves off his hands.

"Would you like a drink of fruit punch?" she called out.

"Yes, please."

Marra went inside and poured her father a glass of the soft-pink punch and picked up her own before walking the short distance to the high well-tended hedge that surrounded the private garden. Marra had only been in the glade once since returning home. She had tried to meditate but had found that there were now too many memories and distractions pulling her focus.

Evannderth took the proffered glass and led her to the bench that faced the magnificent statue of a woman in a feather cloak, holding a baby. Her mother. Marra missed Kahlahnni terribly. That warm, kind presence. The house felt empty and dull without her in it.

"Your dreams are bothering you?" Her father spoke bluntly. It was not typical of him, but when the occasion warranted it, he did not hesitate. Evan tended to be patient and willing to let you decide if you wanted to discuss something with him.

"Yes," Marra admitted. She hadn't had a restful sleep in so long; she probably couldn't even tell him when it had been. At this point, she had reached a vicious cycle of longing for sleep and dreading sleep in equal measure. She hummed herself to sleep in the hope that would ease the dreams. Evan had also sung her to sleep and continued while she slept until he had no voice left, but neither held the dreams at bay for long.

"I am here for you. Talk to me," he urged her. "Has the dream changed?"

"Yes and no." Marra continued to look up at the stunning statue of her mother. She wondered what Kahlahnni was doing at that moment. *She must be going crazy by now not knowing if I have survived.* "Do you think Mum knows I am alive?"

"Without a doubt," Evannderth answered immediately. "There is not a chance she would not have come through that portal by now if she wasn't certain you lived. She may not know what has occurred and that you are doing well, but she does know you survive. I am sure of that."

Marra nodded, more to herself than to anything her father had said. "I dream of the same things I did the night before the Challenge. Assassins, ships, changing Brands, a missing shoe, a shattered throne, and both Harley and Tom dead."

"But?" Evannderth prompted.

"There is now a black cloaked figure standing in the shadows, behind the shattered throne, under the ever-changing symbols, and they hold a large gold ring that has several old style skeleton keys."

Evan nodded as he took in what she was saying. "Do you get any particular feelings from him or is it much of the same sensations of warning and danger?"

Marra considered the question. "To be honest, I have been far more interested in trying to see who he is, so if I see him when we return I will know."

"I wanted to talk to you about you returning to Segarris, your recovery and what would happen if you don't go back."

He took a sip of the punch and Marra waited, but he said nothing further. She couldn't stand the silence so asked, "Are you not worried about getting back soon? We don't know why the assassins are in my dreams. Will they come for you or mother this time, or will there be another attempt on me or Harley?"

"That's what I wanted to talk to you about. Your mother's powers are fully functioning, and her visions should now be clearer as the decision for who will rule has finally been decided. Harlonngraith's coronation will be coming soon, and I need to be there. You are healed, but need time to regain your strength and are certainly not ready to face assassins if they come again."

She heard the concern in his voice and couldn't ignore it. "Harley will need my support. He has much he wants to change." Marra tried to make him understand.

Evannderth put his now-empty glass on the bright green grass and turned to face Samarra. "I don't want you to think about Harlonngraith and what he needs. I want you to think about what you need. Take some time and consider your future. You almost died for him and Segarris, it was only by the skill of the priest that you are still here."

Marra nodded as he spoke. All he said was true, but it didn't make her decision any easier. "You will return to Segarris for good?" she asked. "Regardless of my decision?"

"Yes. Your mother and I have spoken about it at length. We have duties that need to be seen to. Harlonngraith will need help as he tries to navigate being a new king, and having his mother and Lady Darria still seeking revenge will certainly test him. There is also the matter of your dreams and whatever your mother has been experiencing and I personally want to resume my study of the Brands and if there is something wrong with the ceremony."

"That is a lot to take on," she noted.

This made him laugh. "Yes. It is time to return and pick up our duties. You are all we had hoped you would be, but I am a soldier and it is time for me to serve my king."

"You would abandon me here?"

He raised a blond eyebrow at her but didn't scoff at her words; instead he took her hand. "You are eighteen. Grown up enough to choose to marry and follow a man and fight for a nation. No one is abandoning you, we have simply come to a crossroads where as adults we must make our own decisions for our own lives. We are telling you that we think you are remarkable and absolutely capable of choosing your own path. You have played your role as Champion and paid a hefty price. Now the decision you make regarding your future will be completely without our influence."

Evan smiled gently and gave her hand a little squeeze before letting it go. He retrieved his glass from the ground and took her now-empty one. "Just think about it. There are still a few more days before I return." He walked out of the perfect hedged garden area, and it was only then that Samarra realized the sun was beginning to set.

She stood and looked around the glade, her eyes falling on the tree she had been avoiding looking at. With a sigh of frustration, she made her way over to the long-limbed branches and came to stand at the broad trunk. Marra ran her fingers over the mark where the blade had landed when she had thrown it at Harlonngraith in a fit of rage when he had revealed his true identity and she had thought he was simply making fun of her and trying to break up with her. She thought about it now and recalled how quickly the anger had boiled up and made her throw the stunning blue blade. Marra had accidentally nicked Harley's upper arm and Evan had had to sew him up. Her fury had made her sloppy. Her hand dropped away from the scar in the bark of the tree, and she leaned forward and pressed her forehead against it. Silent tears fell as she looked inside herself to face the person she was. Rage and fury made her impulsive and dangerous, a person she didn't like being. And yet focused and calculated, as she had been on the floor of the Arena facing Shai, had made her deadly, which in some ways was even worse. It was a side of her she was yet to reconcile. Twice she had killed men and twice she didn't regret it. What did that make her?

Should she stay here and try to find peace on this beautiful property and run her father's dojo? Ignoring the dreams that plagued her, hoping that once the situation in Segarris resolved one way or another that the dreams would leave her. She knew her heart would always remain with Harley, but there was no danger here and no chance of her having to take another person's life again. Or should she return and take her place as a Soul Sleeper and offer aid to the nation that she had come to love, and sit by Harlonngraith's side as his queen?

Chapter 9

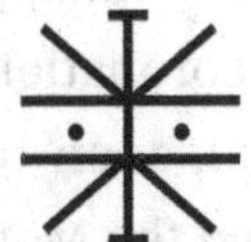

Harlonngraith

The narrow, long, wooden rod was planted in the center of the semicircle of low lying metal bowls that each held a fire he had lit upon arriving. He took a moment to study the head of the rod as the two times he had been in the room prior there had been other concerns and a need for haste. At the top of the rod sat two gold prongs with a large sparkling gem between them. He wondered what it was for and made a mental note to ask the few people who knew about this room if they had any idea what its use was.

Dismissing the rod as there was nothing he could ascertain from it, he looked to the archway that was blocked by brick, giving the impression that the room was a dead end. As he moved closer to the wall, he could make out the eight brands that made up the caste system of Segarris. He noted the lower castes of the Servant and Commoner, as well as the Pomaikkan, or more commonly known as Roamer Brand. There were also the Religious, Warrior, and Noble Brands. Leaving only two. The rarest Brands. The Gifted Brand, which was for the first time in living memory being worn by more than one person at a time. And the final Brand that was only ever worn by one person at a time, the one that could have cost him everything. The Monarch Brand, which he would receive in three days when his coronation would occur.

Prince Harlonngraith, soon to be King of Segarris, reached out and touched the Monarch symbol. He felt it pulsate and instantly a bright white light glowed within the palm of his hand. Curiously he pressed his palm firmly onto the upraised Brand and watched the light from his palm infuse the symbol underneath it. The Brand slowly moved out from under his hand and began to move in a circular pattern.

"I would suggest you remove your hand, Your Highness," a pleasant female voice said from behind him.

Instantly he pulled his hand away and turned to face the Seer, who happened to also be his mother-in-law. Harlonngraith attempted to keep the guilty look from his face—after all, he was the one in charge.

This just made Kahlahnni laugh. "Clearly you're anxious to see who comes through, but opening a portal to another realm without anyone else here is probably not advisable. Wouldn't you agree?"

Harlonngraith smiled at the soft admonishment. "Why are you always so sensible?"

"Because someone has to be." Her tone was light, no condescending attitude he would have got from his mother if she were in this situation. He always felt like he was disappointing her and she was exasperated with his choices, and it would be best for everyone if he stood aside and let her do it. Kahlahnni, on the other hand, made the same observations but in a gentle, kind manner that made him feel young and unlearned, not stupid and incompetent.

Harlonngraith looked over the beautiful Pomaikkan's shoulder to see Arch Deacon Zussya smiling with a look that clearly told the prince he was staying out of this discussion. "Do you think I could open it by myself?" he asked, turning back to the bricked in archway.

"Most likely," admitted Kahlahnni. "But let us not play around with it just now. Though, perhaps later once this is done."

"It is something I would like to witness if at all possible?" Zussya finally spoke since entering the room.

The Seer moved aside and allowed the Arch Deacon to stand beside her. "My family will forever owe you a debt of gratitude." She inclined her head toward the overweight, heavy bearded priest. "After all, you were the one to lead us to this place and help us escape. If you wish to witness if the King can open the portal, I, for one, will not deny it."

Arch Deacon looked fondly at Kahlahnni before he turned to Harlonngraith. "I am surprised to see you here. When I got word from Lahnni that she had a vision that it was time for Evan to return, I thought it would just be the two of us."

Harlonngraith nodded. "I got the same message."

Twice Harlonngraith went to speak and each time he stopped himself. It was like he was hoping if he didn't speak the words the chance of it happening would not be brought into reality. He knew it was silly, he had no say nor influence over what was to come, but he didn't want to hex it. The Seer's wording had bothered him since receiving the note. She had only mentioned Evan's return.

"I don't know." The Seer spoke into the silence of the room. She looked at him with her stunning brown eyes, so much like her daughter's that it made his heart heavy. He missed Samarra more than he thought possible.

"You don't know, what?" he asked.

"If she will return to you."

"You can read my mind?"

"No, I have told you many times that unless I am touching you I can't know your thoughts, but if I let my shield down or the emotions are intense enough, I can feel what others around me do. And I feel your fear."

Harlonngraith didn't deny it. How could he, when it was true? He was terrified that Samarra would choose to stay in her place of birth and not return to be with him. But how could he fault that when she had given up everything for him to gain the throne, and it had almost cost her her life. She had killed for him, and she deserved peace. And there would be no peace. Her dreams would remain disturbed if she lived here as her predictions the night before the Challenge were now confirmed by the Seer's own visions. "You know her better than me," he spoke quietly. "I was hoping you would have some insight into what she will do."

"I know her well," agreed Kahlahnni. "Yet, you have her heart. She has always been her own person. People have often seen her quiet nature as a weakness, never realizing her depth and strength underneath."

"What will you do if she stays behind?"

"Captain Evannderth and I will remain in Segarris. We will not return. We only left to protect Samarra. Our duty has always been to the nation. You will need us as we face whatever is yet to reveal itself. Once you are crowned, things can settle and Evan will start to re-establish his spy network and I will head to Ohanelle with the note you have regarding Marra's dream and see what Heiranni and Lopakka can glean from it."

He frowned. "You will leave her on her own?"

Kahlahnni studied him a moment longer before casting her eyes to the darkened corner and back again. "Would she be alone though?"

"I am sorry to interrupt the both of you, but should we not be getting started?" Arch Deacon Zussya looked anxiously toward the closed door. "I don't like being down here for long periods of time. Each time we are here we run the risk of being discovered. And while I am all for coming back and seeing if the king can open the portal by himself, his movements are under great scrutiny at the moment."

"True," Kahlahnni calmly agreed.

Harlonngraith was coming to appreciate how unruffled she appeared regardless of what was going on around her. He hoped to emulate that as he learned the finer points to ruling well.

"I am the one that called you here, so it stands to reason that I be the one to decide when it is time to open the portal. Agreed?" Though her tone was again light, there was no mistaking who controlled events in this room.

Harlonngraith hid his grin by compressing his lips as he watched Zussya pretend to glower at the diminutive woman. These two clearly had a great respect for each other and the priest was possibly one of the few people not cowed by Kahlahnni's great gift. He knew his role and place in Segarris and was not threatened by her as many other council members had been showing since her return.

Zussya had more power and influence than most on the council with Queen Anzhellika and was proving to be just as relevant to Harlonngraith. This put him in an enviable position, and the prince surmised the priest didn't need to covet Kahlahnni's position because he had his own. At its core, this was what politics was—people jostling for enough power to influence the one with the true power. And the one with the true power being able to understand the motives of the ones attempting to influence him. Which was why it was imperative to understand each member of his council and what their real motives were. He had secretly considered having each council member submit to a meeting with the Seer to have a reading, be damned with ethics, but in the end Harlonngraith knew it was wrong on many levels.

To break the silence and also attempt to distract himself of his racing thoughts of whether his Bonded was going to return to him, Harlonngraith spoke to both of them. "I was thinking of elevating Captain Evannderth to the rank of General when he returns. What are your thoughts?"

"Splendid. He deserves it," Zussya agreed immediately.

"I think that is something best left for him to decide," countered Kahlahnni. "There are pros and cons to being a Captain and a General. Have a private discussion with him and tell him your ideas."

"I wanted him to know how much I appreciate all he has sacrificed for his nation."

She reached out and squeezed his arm, being careful not to touch his skin, Harlonngraith noted. "He knows."

"I hope you both know."

"We do." Kahlahnni smiled up at him and he watched as her eyes lost focus for a brief second.

"It's time," she announced, and without further conversation, let go of his arm and walked to the brick wall.

Harlonngraith watched as Kahlahnni placed her hand flat on the Gifted symbol and as had happened to him earlier an incandescent white light glowed between her hand and the wall. He was fascinated as the Gifted symbol moved out from beneath her hand and slowly began to move in a circle around her hand, inching its way wider and pulling in the other symbols as it came in contact with them. As its speed built, and the circling Brands widened, the light became brighter, causing Harlonngraith to blink. This was the only time he had watched the process, as the first time he had been in this room the portal had been opened from the other side. The second time he had been preoccupied with making certain Samarra continued to breath until she got through the portal and her father could get her to a hospital.

Between one blink and the next, a void formed and the light faded. Kahlahnni took several steps back, allowing room for whoever was about to come through.

Harlonngraith tensed, trying to keep his emotions under control. *Please let her return to me*, he silently prayed, over and over.

In the next heartbeat, Evannderth stepped through carrying two large bags and a backpack. "Well, isn't this quite the welcoming committee? Possibly the three most powerful people in the country, all here to greet little old me." His eyes sparkled at his own joke. Everyone knew the soon-to-be king, while happy to see him, was not putting everything at risk of exposure just to greet his father-in-law.

Kahlahnni kissed Evannderth hello in greeting, but turned quickly back to the void. "I expected a little more from my wife than a cursory kiss," he said mildly, dumping his bags on the floor.

"Harley is not the only one anxious to know what decision she has made," Kahlahnni said, her eyes not leaving the portal void.

"She awaits him on the other side," Evan announced, giving nothing away.

Harlonngraith did not need to be told twice. He took the few steps, and without hesitation, stepped through the void.

There she stood. Healed and whole, and Harlonngraith noted she was standing in between two huge bags, just like her father's. He let out a huge whoop and went to sweep her up into his arms but stopped just in time, realizing that hugging her hard was not the best decision for broken ribs. Instead, he hugged her gently before leaning down to kiss her. She tasted of chocolate. "Are you really doing this?" he whispered.

"If you pick up these bags for me I will," she whispered. "I can't carry anything that heavy." Samarra leaned down and picked up the small backpack and slung it over her shoulder. "This is all I am allowed for a few more weeks."

Harlonngraith didn't wait; he picked up the bags and took a quick look around the bookshop to make certain no one could see them, but like always, the last row of bookshelves with its mirror at the end of it, remained unseen. "You first," he urged. "Your mum is waiting to see you too."

His beautiful Bonded reached up and caressed his cheek. "I love you." Her words were soft, but the meaning hit him hard. She was about to step away from her life forever for him.

He swallowed around the lump in his throat as he watched her step into the mirror. With a final glance to make sure they weren't seen, he followed Samarra through to be met by tears on the other side. Both women were crying as they were reunited.

"Lahnni, you need to close the portal," Evannderth pointed out after a few more minutes of hugging and after the crying had stopped.

The Seer arched an eyebrow at Harlonngraith and then at Zussya. "Let's see if the King can do it."

"What do I do?" asked Harlonngraith as he looked dubiously at the large void in the archway.

"Look closely at the border of the archway," she instructed.

Harlonngraith did what he was told and moved to the opening. There he noticed the symbols that represented the eight Brands were on the raised edging of the curved arch. Four on each side. The Monarch sat at the top of one side, while the Gifted Brand was at the top of the other. He raised his hand and placed it on the Monarch Brand and felt it pulsate, but unlike the first time, a bright white light did not appear. He frowned but didn't remove his hand. "What am I doing wrong?"

"Nothing. It is harder to close than open," explained Kahlahnni. "Remove your hand for a moment."

Harlonngraith did what he was told.

"Marra, find your Brand and place your hand on it," the Seer continued.

Harlonngraith watched and was surprised to see Samarra reach for the Gifted symbol rather than Warrior one to place her hand upon.

"Good," her mother said. "You understand it is time to put aside that part of you."

"Yes, it is one of the reasons I returned," answered Samarra.

Harlonngraith wondered what that was supposed to mean. He noted that the white light didn't return for Samarra either. And suddenly it was clear. This was about them working together. They were stronger together. He nodded to Kahlahnni showing her he understood as he reached up and placed his hand back up on the Monarch Brand. Every brand exploded into a bright blue light and the pulsating under his palm grew stronger. He looked to Samarra to find her staring at him, her eyes wide with wonder as they worked together.

"Bring your hands towards the center of the portal, as if you are drawing a curtain closed. It will resist you, but you are stronger," Kahlahnni explained.

With Samarra beside him, Harlonngraith knew he could do it, and moving his hand as if he truly held the symbol in his grasp, he pictured a heavy curtain and pulled it across the void to meet Samarra's hand in the center. As his hand moved, he noted the bricks beginning to appear. This gave him the confidence to continue until he touched her hand, and once the brick wall was complete, all the Brands snapped back into place with an audible pop. He dropped his hand with a sigh and blinked as a moment of dizziness swept over him.

Before Harlonngraith's vision cleared, Evannderth took control of the situation. "I am certain you have been missing long enough, Your Highness. Let us enjoy our reunion more properly once you are back in the palace where you should be. Let us not have your mother searching for you."

"It is wise council," Zussya agreed.

Harlonngraith didn't argue, no matter how much he wished he could stop and inspect Samarra and ask her a thousand questions about her recovery. Instead, he picked up her two bags and headed for the door. It was only when he heard Kahlahnni speak did he remember his own bag hastily stowed in the corner and the reason he had arrived earlier in the secret room.

"Zussya could you please pick up the pack in the corner?" she asked as they headed out the door.

"Who's pack is it?" the Arch Deacon asked as he moved to the darkened corner.

"Harlonngraith's."

"And why does he have a bag down here?" the priest asked as he carried it out the room looking from the Seer to the Prince.

"That should be obvious. It would seem that if Samarra had chosen to not come to him, he was going to her."

Chapter 10

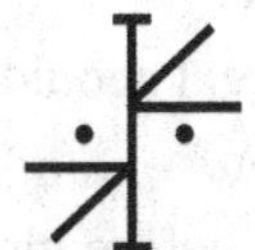

Tommofey

T om had never had people to rely on before, and he occasionally still had moments of self-doubt that they weren't really his friends. They were only being nice because they either felt sorry for him or were too worried about the ramifications as he was still a prince. His title had not been stripped—yet. He paused at the barrack doors and gathered his courage. Today, after his meeting with his mother, he was feeling vulnerable and had instinctively headed toward the perceived comfort of the warriors' quarters rather than the solitude of his private quarters.

He and his mother had been building up to this confrontation for a few days and it had finally come to a head when Darria had announced that she was sending a note on the morrow declining Harlonngraith's invitation to his coronation on both of their behalf.

"Of course, I am going." Tommofey's tone had been sharp. He had had enough of his mother's demands over the last few weeks. Her voice had become shrill and grating and he was actually looking forward to going to the palace and pledging allegiance to Harlonngraith, if for no other reason than to get away from her complaining.

"That is ludicrous," she had gasped with a little too much drama in her tone.

"He allowed me to live. I should show my gratitude by attending his coronation."

"You already kneeled before him at the Arena. I doubt it is necessary to do it again," Darria had pointed out.

Tommofey had silently counted under his breath to keep his temper in check before answering. "The decision has already been made."

"I am simply trying to help you, just as I have always done." Lady Darria's tone had softened, and she reached across the table to pat his hand in a motherly gesture. "I thought you would do me the good service of showing me your support and remaining here with me while the coronation was performed."

"Why would you need support at that time?"

"Your memory is short."

And yours is too long, he thought to himself. "My memory is fine. It's my continued existence and not being removed from our family home that is making me want to go and show my appreciation and allegiance."

Lady Darria had stared at him a few moments longer than were comfortable, but he refused to be cowed. He knew Aviva would have insisted he go, so he was.

"What are you waiting for?" Griggory yelled as he ran by, interrupting Tommofey's thoughts. "Your Highness, it is about to rain."

Since having to take care of Tom after the death of Aviva and Shai with Tom being in an almost catatonic state the entire trip home, his Page had become more accustomed to speaking his mind. Still recovering from the life-altering events at the Arena, Tom now spent most of his time either in his room burying himself in his cartography work or out in the barracks talking to Captain Albertinne or sparring with *Rank Prynnan. Griggory also took part in the sparring. His opponents were usually the newly Branded Warriors who were assigned this posting due to their heritage. Griggory yanked the heavy door open and stood aside to let the prince through.

"Prince Tommofey, I am surprised to see you here today. With the weather having turned, I thought you would be in front of your fireplace with your map stuff." Pynnan happened to be walking by and greeted him.

"I am a little on edge. Too many things on my mind to sit quietly. I think I need to hit something."

Prynnan laughed. "Then you have come to the right place." The soldier that could have been Tom's Champion if he hadn't have lost to Shai in the tournament, looked down at the young boy, who was doing his best to remain still. "They are learning how to fletch arrows, if you are interested?"

Griggory looked eagerly at Prince Tommofey. "Go ahead. I am certain I can take care of myself for a turning or two."

"Thank you." The skinny boy bowed quickly before dashing off to the section where the newest recruits were housed.

"Stick, fist, or sword?" Pynnan looked expectantly at Tom.

"Sorry?"

"You said you wanted to hit something. I am asking what with? A stick, fist or sword?"

"Oh." Tom frowned as he thought through the options. "Fist?"

"Excellent choice. Giving something a good pummelling can certainly help with stress. This way."

Tommofey followed Pynnan through several large corridors before they came to an open door. There was no one inside the room as they entered, and Pynnan closed it behind them. In five rows of five stood padded dummies with their wooden arms sticking out to the sides on every second one, on the other ones their arms were sticking out the front. "What's with the different arms?" Tom asked as he walked around one of the padded dummies.

"The ones with their arms out to the side are great for practicing landing a punch and learning where to place it. The ones with their arms forward are excellent for learning to duck and weave while still landing punches."

Prince Tommofey used the arms of one of the dummies to hang his coat and jacket on. He rolled up the sleeves of his gray linen shirt and slipped his polished shoes and hose off.

"Would you like to just punch something for a while, or some instruction first?" Pynnan asked.

"Punch first. Instruction second."

"Very well." The warrior inclined his head and moved away from the dummy. "Any particular reason you want to wallop something today?"

"Mother," Tom grunted as he balled up his fist and hit the padded dummy in its midsection.

"Ah," was all the comment Pynnan made.

"Coronation," Tom hit it again, this time with his other hand. It felt good to get his frustration out on something that he didn't have to consider its feelings or the ramifications of his actions. Everything in his life had consequences.

"You are going?" Pynnan didn't seem surprised.

"Yes. I must do the right thing or risk looking ungrateful. People already don't like me because I challenged Harlonngraith in the first place. I have drawn out the nation not having a king for several years, by issuing the Right to Rule, and mother has been leading a quiet campaign against her sister for years." Tom waved his hand at Pynnan as if to dismiss the implications of what he had just said. "But you know all this." He grimaced at him before bringing his fists up to face the dummy. "Even if I don't mean it, I need to go and show the nation that Harlonngraith pardoning me was not a mistake." Tommofey hit the dummy in the chest several times and he noted that it hurt his hands. Maybe this wasn't such a good idea; he didn't want to damage his hands too much and not be able to draw later.

"Do you mean it?" asked Pynnan, his voice quiet.

This gave Tommofey pause. Did he mean it? Was he grateful for having his life spared? "Depends on the day," he finally answered.

"Fair enough."

Pynnan didn't push and Tommofey was grateful. He didn't want to think, let alone talk about how he felt most of the time. It was best to remain in control of his emotions by concentrating on the safe things to discuss with those closest to him. He couldn't bear to talk about her to anyone—even saying her name aloud caused his heart to race and his voice to break. So, he buried himself in his map-making and hitting things that couldn't hit back and tried to find ways to honor her and do better. And that meant going to his brother's crowning ceremony and pledging allegiance to him.

Chapter 11

Samarra

The butterflies in Marra's stomach were not fluttering prettily, they were making a stand and causing anarchy as she waited for the signal that she was to enter the throne room to swear fealty to the newly-crowned and Branded King of Segarris. She had so far managed to remain in the background since her return, which suited the story that she had not been seen as she was convalescing from the near-death injuries she had sustained in the Arena.

Even at the coronation itself, Marra had managed to hide in plain sight by wearing a concealing floor-length cloak and standing behind her mother and father, who took most of the spotlight when people weren't watching Harlonngraith. Unless she was introduced to someone, most people had no idea who the tall, pretty, young woman was standing near the Seer. Her mother stood out with her unusual glossy, black-feathered cloak draped across her shoulders and her gorgeous dark brown curls piled high on her head with three matching black feathers with several diamonds down each shaft pinned into the curls. Marra had been relieved to find her mother had taken care of choosing a ballgown for her.

Now the time had come to step out of the shadows. Marra had been second-guessing her decision to return ever since it had become clear that Harley had no intention of allowing her to swear fealty with her parents. She was to be the last to kneel before the new king. He wanted every person present to see her and know her, and hiding behind Kahlahnni and Evannderth was not acceptable.

Marra had been herded into a room with the other higher-ranking nobles and priests of each order and given refreshments, while those of the lower ranks within the nobility and rich merchants were first presented to swear their allegiance to King Harlonngraith, first of his name. Once they had been ushered through the process, the group, including Samarra, her parents, Queen Anzhellika, and Arch Deacon Zussya had been brought into the waiting area where, in order of importance and rank, had been announced and then allowed entrance into the massive room.

The room was now empty, aside from herself, as the doors were closed on the backs of her parents. They had chosen to be presented together, showing the nation that they were still a united front and one was not more important than the other, regardless of titles. It had caused quite a stir when Harley had insisted that they be presented after his own mother. All he would say to his council members was that he had his reasons.

As Marra waited, she moved to the mirror and untied the cloak she had been wearing all day and handed it to a maid, revealing her unique gown for this momentous occasion. It had a shining polished silver armor-plated bodice, with an intricate raised pattern of the Gifted, Warrior, and Noble symbols upon it. Across her shoulders were beaded stiff shoulder pads with soft sky-blue chiffon sleeves cuffed at the wrists. Her free-flowing skirt was made of layers of fine tulle with more pale blue chiffon over the top and finished with silver and dark-blue beaded Brands in the same pattern as the bodice armor around the hemline. Samarra noted the maid's eyes widened. "It is the most beautiful thing I have ever seen," the maid said in a hushed voice.

"You are going to turn the court on its head in that," a male voice interrupted the moment a tall young man strode through a side door. His voice was mild, but there was an undertone she couldn't place.

"Is that a good or bad thing?" Marra found herself asking.

He looked her up and down in more of a superior movement than a sexual way and casually shrugged. "I guess that will depend on the statement you are trying to make by wearing it."

"What statement do you think it makes?" She was now curious. Her mother had had the stunning dress made while Marra was still recovering from her surgery. Kahlahnni had said that she wasn't certain if Marra would return but wanted to be prepared for any eventuality.

"Warrior Queen," he stated. Marra could not decide if it was a compliment or not. "That you are not to be messed with, and yet there is a regal undertone to the whole thing. Clever use of using three Brands. Shows your parentage as well as your own Warrior one."

Marra didn't disagree with him as he couldn't tell she had more than one Brand with the cuffed sleeves of her gown. "Well, that is astute."

"The one thing I do know is court statements."

He said it in a way that was clearly self-deprecating. Samarra wondered who this tall, well-spoken, handsome man was. He looked like Harley and his brother, and she wondered if he was a distant cousin. He felt familiar but couldn't place him. "Is that the only thing you know?" she asked.

He laughed a short, sharp bark. "Look at you making conversation with the enemy."

"Sorry?" she asked, taken aback by his words.

The double doors were swung open and the Master of Ceremonies announced in a clear voice, "Prince Tommofey, the third."

"Oh, and I know maps." He sniffed at her in a haughty manner that made her scowl before he inclined his head and walked to the door and into the chatter that had spread quickly around the room when his name had been announced.

The doors were pulled closed again and Marra looked over at the maid who seemed to have the same stunned look on her face that Marra guessed was on her own. "That was unexpected." She said it more to herself than the few servants and guards in the room. She had been dreaming about Tom as well as Harlonngraith for months, how had she not recognized him?

The maid nodded but didn't add anything. You didn't comment on the royal family regardless of how estranged it was.

Marra hated to admit it, but she was shaken by finding out who the man was. She turned to look in the mirror, pretending to check her appearance for the final time, when all she was truly trying to do was distract herself from the feeling of guilt slowly washing over her. Tommofey had lost so much and she had been instrumental in that. She lifted her hand to pat her blonde hair in place, but brought it back down when she noted it trembling slightly. *You're going to be fine*, she told herself. *You did what you had to do to keep Harley alive.* She took several deep breaths, repeating the words in her head and finding her center like she had been shown.

By the time the double doors swung open to admit her, she had her nerves under control and a look of determination plastered on her face. She heard her full name announced but paused as the words registered fully to her and everyone in the audience chamber. Samarra Kahlahnni Cellecia Durrand Vissermonte The words reverberated around the room as everyone looked in awe at her. The Master of Ceremonies had just told everyone that the rumor she had been Bonded to the King was true by adding the royal family's last name to her own already distinguished names.

Without prompting, row after row of the most influential people in the nation stood to honor her. Marra gave a tight-lipped nervous smile to the ones closest to her before lifting her head and meeting eyes with the man waiting at the end of the long aisle. She kept her eyes firmly on him as she walked passed the now-silent stunned crowd. Harlonngraith looked spectacular and regal sitting on the huge throne in his ermine robe, dyed the same color blue as her dress, a heavy silver crown on his head embellished with diamonds and sapphires. She didn't realize how perfectly their court clothing would match until this moment.

Her broad-shouldered, sharp-jawed king with his shaggy light brown hair smiled encouragingly at her as she reached the bottom of the dais. Not waiting for any aid, she lifted her skirts and walked up the three steps to stand before the king. Marra went to curtsy, but Harley spoke steadily into the silence. "No." His voice rumbled across the room. Her heart always fluttered when he used that tone. "I told you once, long ago, that you should never bow to me and I meant it."

Loud gasps filled the hall as King Harlonngraith did the unprecedented and stood and knelt before Samarra. "I will forever be indebted to you for being my Champion. Segarris owes you for making me a better king and seeing beyond my own nose." He stood and took her hand. Harley turned them both toward the astounded crowd. "The Seer has warned of many challenges to come, but today we celebrate the ending of uncertainty and look ahead to forge a new beginning that will hopefully re-unite us all."

And with those words, the assembled audience erupt-ed into enthusiastic applause. Marra continued to smile throughout the announcement, but worried about what was to come. While Harley had been busy planning the coronation and the changes to tradition and trying to keep them all secret, Marra had been keeping her own choices to herself and it was almost time to reveal them.

Harlonngraith

I t was done. He was king. It had taken years longer than it should because of Tommofey's Right to Rule Challenge being issued, but it was over. Harlonngraith had survived by the lethal skill and intelligence of his Bonded and had almost lost her in the process. But they both lived, and it was done.

No more uncertainty. His mother thought him a fool, though she had used harsher words, for pardoning his brother and allowing him to live. Harlonngraith had tried to point out on several occasions that if the Gods were unhappy with his choice, they would not have allowed Tommofey to leave the Arena after the Challenge had been completed. It had been made abundantly clear when he and Samarra had entered through the tunnel that there was no turning back. Now he was about to make his mother miserable and shock those assembled by having a short private meeting with him.

Harlonngraith nodded and murmured thanks to several fawning nobles who had stopped to engage him in conversation and offer their congratulations. Samarra stood by his side, and he could feel her unease as she smiled and accepted praise for her extraordinary fighting skills. All this attention was making her uncomfortable; she was shy and didn't like crowds and here she was, standing beside him the center of everyone's focus with a mass of people wanting to talk to her.

"I am terribly sorry to interrupt, Your Majesty." Kahlahnni approached, her husband by her side. "But there is someone who would like to meet Lady Samarra."

Harlonngraith smiled graciously at the baron and his wife as they politely excused themselves. He turned to his mother-in-law. "Thank you." He took Samarra's hand and squeezed it reassuringly. "You are doing so well. It can be overwhelming if you are not used to it."

"You have no idea. Is there a tower here I could lock myself in with a good book and just leave you to it?" Samarra joked, though Harlonngraith got the impression it was only half in jest. She turned to the Seer. "I don't know how you do it, Mum. I am struggling with all these people. How you cope with all their emotions as well must be overwhelming."

"Practice, my beautiful girl. Lots of hours with Heiranni pushing to keep me balanced and centered. The Right to Rule Challenge was far more difficult with all those heightened emotions and what could be described as a blood lust being aroused in many. Violence is far more difficult to process and keep at bay than the relief and joy that today brings." Kahlahnni inclined her head toward Harlonngraith before leaning gently on her husband. "These two also help as they both have superior control over their emotions, making being around them a haven when I am amongst a crowd."

This surprised Harlonngraith. "I do?"

"Oh, yes. Probably from the years of training you have received from your tutors and keeping your emotions in check when dealing with your mother and her demands." Kahlahnni kept her voice low. "The only thing that ever rattles you is my daughter," the Seer said knowingly, and then changed the subject. "I believe you have a meeting you asked me to join?"

"Of course. Thank you for the reminder." Harlonngraith looked to Samarra and knew Kahlahnni was correct. She was the only one who could impact his direction, determination, and choices in a profound way. Had he not been willing to walk away from all of this power and riches to spend a simple life with her in the hills of another world? She was his everything and he was going to do anything in his power to make it safe for her, so she need never kill again. They had not spoken of it since her return, but he knew that there had to be some form of trauma attached to the whole thing and he wanted to ease it. "I need to take this quick meeting. Would it be all right if I left you with your father to continue representing us?" he asked Samarra.

"Yes, I'll be fine. I am being dramatic."

"Don't push yourself. You are still healing," Evannderth reminded her. He turned to his wife. "You go do what you need to with the new king, and once you return, I think it's time we took our leave and Marra can join us and no one will dare to comment."

"I'll need to stay a while longer," admitted Harlonngraith.

"Arch Deacon Zussya can stand with you to help with difficult hangers on," suggested Samarra.

"Good idea." He nodded. "I won't be long." Harlonngraith bent and kissed Samarra's cheek and whispered, "Love you."

"Love you more," she whispered back.

Harlonngraith grimaced as he stood and offered his arm to the Seer. "Let's get this done."

Kahlahnni took his arm, and they moved through the crowd. The celebrations were in full swing, though everyone was still very much on their best behavior. The large orchestra played slower music and a few couples had taken to the designated dance floor. Harlonngraith noted that the mood as mentioned by the Seer was definitely more of a relief and guarded optimism rather than carefree joy.

"You are being very secretive about who we are meeting," Kahlahnni noted as she nodded and smiled at people who moved out of their way.

"Not secretive, more that I didn't want to add to Samarra's worries. We are meeting Tommofey, and I wasn't sure how she would feel about it. I have been avoiding anything that may upset her," he explained.

"And you want me to be there because?" she asked.

He raised his eyebrows at her. "You aren't surprised that I am meeting my brother?"

Kahlahnni laughed as they reached the corridor and several guards fell in place around them. "There is little in this world that surprises me, and you would not be you if you didn't take this chance to connect with the man you pardoned."

"Your Majesty, he is in here, as you requested." One of his personal bodyguards indicated a door to the left.

"Thank you. I will only require one of you to enter and stand by the door."

Harlonngraith opened the door and stood aside, allowing the Seer to step through first. They were followed by the single guard who closed the door and took his position in front of it, his hand resting on his sword hilt.

"Prince Tommofey, thank you for agreeing to meet with me." Harlonngraith began the conversation, trying to keep his tone light. This was the first time in their lives they had been in the same room and able to converse without their mothers glowering at each other.

"I didn't deem it wise to disregard a request from my king." He looked around the room. "What is this place? I always assumed the palace library would be larger."

"It is the private library of the royal family." Harlonngraith looked around. "I don't think mother ever bothers to come in here." He wrinkled his nose as he took in the old worn desk in the corner and a faded lounge sitting in front of an empty fireplace that looked like it hadn't been lit in decades. Several low side tables were filled with trinkets, and by the heavy drawn curtains sat a high-backed chair with matching footstool. A massive map covered the length of one wall and sat above the fireplace. The other two walls held floor-to-ceiling book-shelves stuffed with books, scrolls, folded parchment, and other odds and ends. The door sat in the center of one of the shelves. "If you did ever wish to visit the palace library that could be arranged." He returned his gaze to his halfbrother.

Prince Tommofey inclined his head.

"Allow me to formally introduce to you Kahlahnni Dur-rand, the Seer of Segarris." Harlonngraith watched Tom-mofey and noted he didn't recoil at the woman. Instead, he bowed deeply, being careful to keep his hands behind his back.

"Prince Tommofey, it is a pleasure to meet you, and though I am uncertain if you wish to hear this from me, may I offer my condolences and say I am sorry for your loss."

The prince's eyes widened at her words, and for a brief moment, Harlonngraith thought he saw the depth of grief his brother was experiencing. But too quickly his face resumed its slightly haughty appearance. "And I would like this opportunity to offer my apologies for what my mother did to you. She has no remorse, but I find her choices on occasion to be extreme."

Harlonngraith cleared his throat. "While we are choos-ing to speak candidly, allow me to ask you a question."

"Go on," said Tommofey.

"If you had become king, what would you have done to improve this country?"

Tommofey didn't hesitate. "The Branding Ceremony."

Harlonngraith hid his surprise. "In what way?"

"It has come to my attention that there may be an issue with people being Branded incorrectly. I would be looking into that." His words held pain, but Harlonngraith didn't understand why.

"Obviously something you have thought through." He chose his words carefully. "Well, clearly you are not an imbecile."

Tommofey continued to watch him but made no comment.

"And smart enough to hold your tongue." Harlonngraith came to his decision quickly. "If I offered you a position on the council, would you take it?"

"If it is offered in genuine want to change and to build a better future then I would indeed consider it."

"Really?" Harlonngraith raised his eyebrows at him. "That easy? We have been raised to hate each other and you would serve me?"

"Oh, I admit it leaves an odd taste in my mouth, but you intrigue me." Tommofey shrugged nonchalantly. "And I owe you."

"You owe me nothing. Others have controlled our path for too long."

"And you show your defiance and difference from your mother by pardoning me and now appointing me to your council? That is certainly a bold statement."

"Ha, you just apologized to the Seer on behalf of your mother," Harlonngraith retorted, "and you want to investigate one of our most sacred ceremonies. Both quite bold statements too."

They stood there for several moments, assessing each other. Harlonngraith was surprised that he didn't hate his brother. Could it be that it was easier to forgive because he was the victor in this situation?

"It is agreed then?" Kahlahnni asked both of them.

"It would seem so." The prince nodded.

"I must get back, but I expect you here at the beginning of the week for the first council session. Everyone will swear oaths at that time."

"Very well," Tommofey agreed. "I will take my leave of you." He bowed formally and turned to the Seer. "Lady Kahlahnni." He inclined his head and the guard moved aside to allow him to leave.

"Well?" asked Harlonngraith, looking over at the Seer.

"Well, what?" Kahlahnni asked.

"Please don't do that. You are my mother-in-law and the Seer, but I am king and this is important. You know why I asked you to come."

Kahlahnni looked at him seriously. "I was testing you. It is good that you don't allow even me to put you off or make you explain when it is not required. I was worried your mother may have too much of a hold on you and your choices." She smiled at him. "Something I no longer need to be concerned about. You handled that well. Not overly friendly, not arrogant and prickly, and sensitive enough to not rub it in his face that he lost."

"Thank you, but you still haven't answered my question."

This brought out a loud unexpected laugh that reminded Harley of Samarra's laugh when she was comfortable around you. "Oops, sometimes I do get side-tracked. Yes, to your unasked question. I think you did the right thing. If he is trustworthy, you have begun the process of gaining a powerful ally. If he is not to be trusted, it is always best to keep your enemies close."

"My thoughts exactly." As they moved toward the door to rejoin the coronation festivities, he looked over to Kahlahnni. "It was surprising that he brought up the Branding Ceremony."

"Indeed it was."

Chapter 12

Samarra

S he was tired and grateful that the day was over. The ballgown her mother had designed had been magnificent and had been the talk of the coronation gala, but the armor bodice had become heavy after a few hours and had rubbed on the newly healed scars on her ribs until it was painful to shift in certain directions. Samarra's new maid Gallya undid the final part of the lacing in the bodice and Marra let out a relieved sigh. "Free," she announced.

This brought a giggle from the young woman, who was only a few years older than Marra. Gallya quickly helped her out of the rest of the tulle and chiffon concoction and gathered it up as best she could without crushing it. "I will take this to the laundry myself to make certain it is not ruined by some ham-fisted page."

Marra nodded as she pulled on her soft sky-blue robe and belted it at the waist. She kept a straight face at the way Gallya took her role so seriously. It was something Marra was still trying to get used to. All these servants to answer every whim, it now made complete sense why Harley had been proud of himself when he had announced that he washed his own dishes. "Gallya, thank you for your help this evening. You may retire for the night as I am heading straight to bed."

"But your hair?"

"I can deal with my hair. It's only a few pins." She waved her hand toward the door. "Did I not overhear a few of you talking about a party that always happens in the old stables once you have been dismissed from your chores? Would it not have begun by now?"

"Oh, yes, My Lady."

"Then deliver the dress to the laundry, but it is to be left and taken care of tomorrow. I won't be needing it anytime soon. Go enjoy your evening. That is an order." Samarra added a smile to the final statement to let Gallya know she was joking.

Her maid curtsied before heading out the door of the change room that Marra now occupied. Marra plonked down onto the padded stool that sat before the mirror and began to poke around in her hair to find the pins that held her long blonde tresses in place. It didn't take her long and she shook her head for the final piece to fall down her back. The day had been long, and eye-opening in the extravagance surrounding it. But she supposed that's what coronations were—a show of wealth and strength to all. Samarra had to admit that after experiencing today, she was completely out of her depth in planning a royal wedding if Anzhellika was going to continue to insist on one.

"There you are," Harlonngraith announced as he strode into the room. "Pattraic and I have been looking for you."

Pattraic was Harley's oldest servant and a bit of a stickler for protocol, Marra had learned. It was a good and bad thing. It had stopped her from making several silly mistakes that would not have done anything but cause her embarrassment, but she always felt like he was judging her, and she was coming up a little short to be the next queen of Segarris.

"And now you have found me."

"Yes." Harley looked around the opulent room. "Where is Gallya?"

"I just dismissed her. There is a party or something in the old stables and I didn't want her to miss out."

"I forgot about that. Hang on." Harley walked from the room.

Marra finished brushing her hair and opened her robe to apply a salve of tea tree ointment to the scar tissue that was mildly inflamed from the wonderful gown. Harlonngraith came back as she was finishing and he halted, his beautiful gray eyes lingering on her naked body. She noted he looked hungry, and it made her insides clench. They were yet to make love since she had been injured and she was tired of waiting for him to make the first move. Taking her shyness and shoving it down, Marra stood and slowly allowed the robe to slide from her bare shoulders.

Harley licked his lip but didn't move.

Closing her eyes for a moment, she gathered her courage—in some ways this was scarier than stepping into the Arena—and opening her eyes, Marra walked toward her Bonded and reached up to wrap her arms around his neck. She didn't know why she was so nervous. It was like they were starting over.

"Stop," his voice rumbled and Marra looked up at him through her lashes, hoping she looked alluring.

"Why?" she asked softly.

"I don't think this is a good idea."

She kept her voice even as she again asked, "Why?"

"I don't want to hurt you."

"You won't." Without waiting for an answer or giving him the chance to worry further, Marra dropped her arms from around his neck and took hold of the front of his trousers and undid the buttons. She pulled out his cock and held it tightly in her fist, slowly pumping up and down. The groan that escaped his lips was everything. "I am not waiting any longer. I am healed and horny."

This made him laugh and reach up to remove his jacket. Marra didn't stop to watch, instead she knelt and ran her tongue along the underside of his cock, before taking him into her mouth. She could taste the precum and sucked hard on the smooth tip before letting him go to pull his pants and under garments down to the floor to pool at his feet. Marra ran her nails across his arse and drew him into her mouth, sucking and licking while continuing to pump with her hand. She started slow but her urgency and speed grew quickly. Hearing him moan, and knowing she was the reason for it, was intoxicating.

"Marra," he spoke harshly, and somewhere in the back of her mind she realized it was the first time he had used her less formal name. "Now. I have to have you now," he demanded.

Still holding him in her hand, she looked up at him. "Take me," she responded with equal force.

"Get on your hands and knees," he ordered, his voice like thunder, making her move even quicker to obey. She would do anything for him when he used that voice.

She felt him kneel in between her legs and he placed one hand on her hip while the other rested on the small of her back. "Ready?" he growled, resting the tip of his cock against her entrance.

"Yes." She tensed.

"Don't do that," he ordered and let go of her back, sliding his hand up to the nape of her neck. He leaned over and kissed her ear. "You tense and it will hurt. He slowly pushed into her and she relaxed around him. "God, I've missed this." He pushed himself all the way in and Marra bit her lip at the perfect sensation of him filling her.

Harley kissed her ear one more time before he lifted himself off her back and began to move in and out. He coiled her hair around his hand and pulled her head back, while keeping a firm grasp on her hip. Harley's thrusting became harder and faster and Marra pushed back into him, allowing him to fully take control. He pounded into her and she held on, tensing her legs and arms, her enjoyment growing knowing how much pleasure he was getting from this. He pulled her hair tighter, and his fingers dug into her hip while he kept her in place. "You feel so good," he said through gritted teeth before he stilled and she felt him begin to pump his seed into her. Marra tightened her muscles around him and he shuddered. "Holy Hell," he swore as she did it a second time.

He let go of her hair and hip and pulled her up so they were both kneeling. Harley encircled her waist with his arm to help keep her fully upright. He lifted her hair out of the way and tenderly kissed the nape of her neck, making her moan and pushing her hips back.

"What are you doing?" she gasped as he pulled out of her and moved her onto her back.

"Finishing what you started." Harlonngraith didn't explain further, instead he took her nipple into his mouth and bit down on it. This made her lift her chest toward him and press her hips into the carpeted floor. He moved his hand to one of her breasts and began to twirl her nipple and held her in place while he continued to trail kisses down her torso and over her stomach.

Samarra held her breath as he kissed her gently just inches from her clit. She was tightly coiled, and it wasn't going to take much for her to spiral into an orgasm. The first lick of his rough tongue against her swollen and aroused clit made her quiver. "You are beautiful." He breathed the words against her skin and she gasped with pleasure.

He licked her again and again until she was shaking and tense, barely holding herself together as her orgasm teetered on the edge of falling into oblivion and taking all her senses with it. "You are mine," Harley rumbled, and with a final swipe of his tongue, she came, calling his name over and over while she shuddered under him.

Marra didn't know how long they lay there. It was only that she was growing cold that made her finally want to move from the tangle of naked arms and legs they had formed. "Harley, we need to get up." She shook his shoulder, not sure if he was awake.

"Don't want to," he complained.

"I'm cold," she told him.

With a deep sigh, he moved his legs. "Fine, but we only move to the bed. I am too relaxed to do or think of anything at this time."

"Deal."

They didn't speak, but there was a fair amount of giggling as Harley took Marra's hand and dragged her to the huge four poster bed they shared. The duck-feather-filled quilt was thick and luxurious and she was grateful for its warmth as it was colder here than Melbourne. They faced each other, their legs entwined and hands clasped together under the cover. Her hair lay around them, but she made sure none got in his face—there was nothing worse than being itchy from hair tickling you.

"Did your meeting with my mother go well?" she asked, suddenly remembering she had been meaning to ask him since it had been mentioned.

"I met with Prince Tommofey."

"Okay, that is definitely not what I was expecting you to say. How did it go?"

"Actually better than I thought it would. I asked what he would have done if he was king, and his answer was surprising."

"Well, don't leave it there."

Harley grinned and winked, causing her to glower at him. "He said he would investigate the Branding ceremony."

"Now that is a shock. Did he say anything more?"

"No, we were both careful with our wording and didn't give much away. I did offer him a place on my new council though."

"Do you trust him?" asked Marra, surprised at Harlonngraith.

"No. I have no reason to, but I want to. I am hoping you and your Mum will warn me if there is a reason not to," he admitted.

"We are not your lie detectors," she remarked. "Our gifts don't work like that, and I don't want you relying on me for that. What happens if it disappears and I miss something?" Marra felt panicked. There was so much pressure on her. She wasn't sure she was truly cut out for this.

"You are worrying about nothing. I know to not rely on your Gifts and promise I won't force you to do anything you aren't comfortable with. My mother and aunt tried it with your mother and look where it got them."

Marra nodded, her racing heart slowly returning to normal. "Fair enough. Did he accept your offer to be a council member?"

"Yes, he did."

Marra decided to not say anything about her and Tommofey's strange encounter this afternoon. She would let things play out before she made any decisions.

"You were wonderful today, my queen." He leaned toward her and kissed the tip of her nose, clearly trying to change the topic.

"Thank you, but I am not really your queen. Only in the bedroom." She said it lightly, not wanting to start anything.

"But you are my Bonded and I added my surname to yours."

"Your mother has been clear that I was not part of the coronation because I am not the queen and she remains with that title." Samarra tried to keep her frustration with his mother out of her voice. There had been several small incidents where Anzhellika had been quick to point out that she was still the most important female in Harley's life, no matter the sacrifices Marra had made for him. Why couldn't mothers let their male children go? Or was it the power Anzhellika held that she was struggling to relinquish?

"That's absurd," he announced, letting go of Marra's hand and reaching out to rub his thumb along her jawline. "Mother has no right to say those things." He scowled at her which made Marra laugh.

"Don't scowl at me. It's not my doing." She snaked her hand under the blanket and found his armpit exposed while he was continuing to hold her face. She wondered if he was ticklish. This seemed to be the ideal time to find out.

"Then we will just have to get married in all the pomp and ceremony and crown you as queen at the same time."

Her hand froze before she began to tickle him. "What?"

"You don't want to marry me?" he joked. "It may be a little late for that."

"No, it's not that. I am just a bit confused. I assumed your mother was not willing to cut the apron strings. I thought we were married, now you are saying we're not?"

"We are Bonded in the traditions of the Pomaikkan's and I figured if it was good enough for your parents it was good enough for us. But mother may have a point and the king may have to wed in a formal ceremony with priests and all that stuff for you to be considered my queen."

Marra felt queasy at the thought of all the details she would have to learn to organize such a monumental event. She tried not to shudder at the revulsion of the idea. She also quietly loathed that the queen, in her snarkiness, had been right. The perfect solution came to her, and she grinned evilly at him.

"Oh no." He pretended to be scared and backed away from her. "What?"

"I will marry you on one condition."

"Mmmm...go on," his tone was wary.

"You organize it. You, your mother, and my dad."

Harley blinked at her several times. "Huh? What?"

"I didn't come back just for you, though you were the major part. I came back because your Gods gave me a Gift, I assume for a reason, and I still can't control them properly or make sense of what I see most of the time. I made Lopakka a promise that I would return and complete my training. Mother is coming with me."

"Your father can't go?" Harley grimaced. "Not that you need to tell him I said that."

"No, mother says father's role in my upbringing is complete—he had to train me to be your Champion. Now she has to help me become a master at Soul Sleeping. Whatever that looks like." She scoffed.

"I don't want to live without you again. Those weeks you were away were torture."

"Stop being dramatic. It could be worse," she pointed out.

"How?' he demanded.

"You could be Tommofey and have lost everything."

Chapter 13

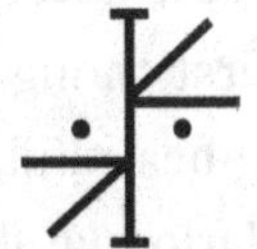

Tommofey

The loneliness was unending. He had more friends now than ever before and yet he felt isolated. Feeling empty or numb would be an improvement than this heart-wrenching, soul-destroying pain. Tommofey doubted he would ever want to feel love again. It was too hard to do more than survive when you lost it.

The nightmares that plagued him weren't helping him find peace either. He continued to dream of Aviva lying in a pool of blood, with Tom standing over her, bloody hands on a bloody knife, and her whispering over and over. "Why did you kill me? I loved you." Every night ended with him tossing and turning until he gave up and lay there staring at the ceiling waiting for the time he could get up and pretend to the world that he was fine.

Today, he lay in bed well past the time he would normally get up, thinking about the day ahead. For once, he was not thinking about Aviva and Shai. Instead, he was trying to decide if he was ready to sit across from his brother and watch him rule. How was he going to feel when he saw Lady Samarra? Was she going to be part of his council? Harlonngraith had made it clear at his coronation that he considered his Bonded his equal.

Tommofey went back to the moment he had come upon Samarra waiting in the antechamber to be presented to the king. Tom's first thought had been how dare she stand there looking beautiful and refined and alive. Spitefully, he wanted Harlonngraith to hurt as much as he did. And clearly her clothing choice had been to remind everyone that under that pretty face was a warrior woman. He had admired her and hated her all in one moment and it was confusing.

"Your Highness, if you don't get up now you are going to be late," Griggory spoke from the doorway.

"And are you ready to go? Got your new uniform on?" Tom pulled himself up to sit against the pillows.

"Yes, got a few funny looks on my way back from the kitchens."

There was a knock on the outer door and Tom frowned. He was not expecting anyone.

"You should get dressed," his Page said boldly. "It is probably your mother."

"My mother? Why?"

"One of the people I ran into was her lady-in-waiting."

Tommofey groaned.

The knock on the door became more insistent.

"Go and answer it. I don't need help getting dressed. Get me tea and a muffin sent up and offer her something." Tommofey didn't wait for Griggory to answer, he pulled the blankets off and stood, stretching his arms over his head.

It didn't take Tom long to get dressed and he was pleased with the result. He wore his usual dark gray trousers and black polished boots, but instead of a white or navy linen shirt he wore one in the palest blue, many would think it white. He wore a tailored vest in his typical navy but through it was a fine sky-blue thread to compliment his shirt. It was a subtle nod to the unity of the sons of King Tommofey but it was clear for those who matter. He ran his hand through his short brown hair and decided a trim was in order.

Giving himself one final check over and a silent word of encouragement, Tom went to tell his mother the news he had been hiding for the last few days.

"Have you lost your senses completely?" Lady Darria demanded as soon as he entered the room.

"Good morning, Mother. Did you sleep well?"

"Passingly well, but that will not deter me from again demanding to know what you think you are doing?"

"What do *you* think I am doing?"

"Making a statement, but to why and who is what I am not understanding."

"After the coronation I had a brief meeting with the king and he invited me to become a member of his council." Tommofey sat and Griggory handed him a cup of tea.

"He did what?"

"Mother, why am I repeating myself?"

"Don't get smart with me, young man. You can't drop this on me and expect me to take it all in and be fine with it. Why have you only told me now?"

"Because I needed time to decide if I was going to go."

"I could have helped you make that decision," she protested.

"I do not mean to appear ungrateful or disrespectful, but you would have said I was insane and tried to talk me out of it."

"That whole family is not to be trusted. You know this. They are the enemy."

Rather than listen to her rant, Tom changed tack. "Do you not think I haven't considered why he asked me? The best way to find out your enemy's weaknesses is to study them. While he studies me, I shall study him. Gaining their trust seems like a completely plausible plan to understanding who they are and how best to be rid of them." He put down his cup and held out his arms. "Wearing this serves a purpose. Like everything else I do. You taught me well, Mother, now trust me."

So far, the first council session had been entirely cordial and civilized. No one had run screaming from the room or protested vehemently against Tommofey being present. There had even been a few nods of greetings as their eyes took in what he wore. As he had told Samarra on Coronation day, he was brilliant at subtle court statements. Anzhellika, his aunt, was the only one who seemed to want to make him feel unwelcome. When their eyes had connected upon him entering the room, she had glared at him before sneering and turning away.

Tommofey was not at all surprised as he guessed his mother would have done the same to Harlonngraith, if not worse.

They had all been sworn in and told that several titles and roles would be distributed after a few sessions were held and once the king had been able to meet with everyone separately. Harlonngraith listed off a few items he would like to cover over the next weeks and told everyone to feel free to come to him with issues they felt needed priority.

Tommofey listened and kept his mouth shut. Six months ago, he would have interrupted, insinuated he was better than most there because his rank was higher, and demanded he sit closer to the king so everyone would know how important he was. Now he understood, thanks to Aviva, that none of that was necessary and just made him disliked. Thinking about her and the profound effect she had had on him in such a short time made him swallow hard against the tears that suddenly threatened to spill. Tom dropped his head and counted to ten, closing his eyes and blocking out what was going on around him while he fought for control of his emotions.

"Are there any further items we should discuss before I close the meeting for today?" Harlonngraith looked around the room.

"I hope this is not too forward of me," a rotund man, with a double chin and thick red beard spoke quietly.

Tom tried to recall his name and where he was from but failed. His mother would be disappointed.

"Will the Seer and the Champion be part of the Council? More women on the council would be a good thing in my wife's opinion."

This brought a smirk to the faces of several men, while a few others scowled. One of the three women present, out of a fifteen-seat council, laughed loudly.

"The queen left for the Pomaikkan Settlement yesterday to complete her training," Harlonngraith answered.

"She is not the queen. She was not included in the coronation ceremony so has spoken no vows of service," Queen Anzhellika interrupted.

The room fell silent and Tommofey, like everyone else, waited to see how Harlonngraith was going to handle his mother. It turned out Tom's aunt was just as difficult as her sister. Since her first glare, he had tried to avoid looking at her, and after this display would double his efforts.

"Training as what?" blurted the red bearded man then turned a bright shade of red at his rudeness.

The King smiled indulgently. "The Lady Samarra has been blessed by the Gods and carry's the Gifted Brand just like her mother."

There were gasps from several people in the room.

"How is that possible?"

"Absolutely unheard of."

"No such thing as having two Brands."

The mutterings continued and Tommofey continued to sit quietly, he had already known about her Gifted brand from the Arena. He still had the note Harlonngraith had given him regarding her dream. It was only now he realized he had never opened it. He wasn't even sure where it was.

A chair scraping along the flagstone floor made everyone turn in their seats. Captain Evannderth stood and there was instant silence. Tom marveled at the response. This man commanded silence by his reputation alone. He should be arrogant and yet his demeanor was reserved and respectful to everyone in the room. Tom's feelings about Evannderth were as mixed as his feelings about his daughter. A towering resentment mixed with anger, but weighed equally with respect and admiration.

He looked around the room, meeting the eye of every one protesting Harlonngraith's words. "My daughter is what the Pomaikkan's call a Soul Sleeper. She developed the ability early, but we weren't in a position to seek help in her training. Kahlahnni has taken her to Ohanelle to complete her studies and see if they can glean any further understanding of the visions they are both experiencing."

Tommofey watched with fascination as the Captain turned to face Anzhellika. "As you have pointed out, there are a few who believe Samarra is not queen, as they were not married in the formal traditions of Segarris. Let us rectify that, so His Majesty can have his queen by his side as he so wishes. My wife and daughter, in their wisdom, have decided the best course of action is to leave the planning up to the experts and then went and dumped it in mine and the king's lap. So, until they return, we have a country to run and a wedding to plan. I have no idea why they would think it a good idea to leave us in charge of the royal wedding but here we are."

This made everyone laugh and Tom noted Evan had cleverly turned the subject onto the wedding and all the things that had to be done and decided—effectively halting Anzhellika's continued remarks about Samarra not being a true queen and moving people on from asking exactly what visions were the two women having. He wondered if he was bold enough to enquire at some point.

Soon after, the council meeting came to a close, and as Tommofey went to leave Harlonngraith approached. "A quick word, brother, if you don't mind?"

Tom could feel everyone watching but didn't look around. "Of course."

He followed Harlonngraith out of a side door, the king's personal guards falling in behind them. They walked down a narrow corridor and passed several more doors before arriving at a plain-looking door. "This is one of the private meeting rooms I had no idea existed until a few weeks ago. No one used them, as Father was always away fighting."

It felt strange hearing Harlonngraith speak about their father in such a familiar tone. Tom felt almost proprietorial about the man.

"There are a few people who I want you to meet. I am forming a small group to look further into what you were discussing the other day."

Tom blinked as he tried to keep up with what Harlonngraith had said without really giving anything away. "Okay."

One of the guards opened the door, and Harlonngraith stepped through, followed by Tommofey. "Hang on," someone called out as the door was shutting. Evannderth slipped through the held door and then it was closed.

"Did you run here?" Harlonngraith asked his father-in-law. "I wasn't expecting you for a little while longer."

"Once I was out of sight, I did manage a swift walking pace. I also cut through the throne room, and managed to startle the window cleaner in the process," he answered jovially, quickly putting everyone at ease.

Neat trick, thought Tommofey. There were two other men in the room and a woman. All three wore cassocks. *Interesting.* He knew one of the men. It was Arch Deacon Zussya. The heavy set, dark bearded priest who had hand-delivered the note from the Seer that set Tommofey on his path to finding his Champion and so much more. The other man was far younger, closer to Tom's age, and though they had never formally met, Tom knew this to be his other half-brother, Platisse. He had been at the coronation of course, but had stayed in the background and amongst the other accolates in attendance. Tom wondered whose decision that was. The only woman in the room was approximately the same age as Zussya and wore a cassock of the finest cloth, but in the teal green of the Sisters of Seggar.

After the brief and slightly awkward introductions, cider was served and a platter of sweet meats brought in as they settled around the small table and waited for Harlonngraith to speak. "I have gathered you all in here in secret in the hope that between us we can discover what, if anything, is happening with the Branding ceremony."

Tom barely kept his surprise in check. Platisse did a poorer job of it. "There is a problem with the Branding ceremony?" the young priest asked.

"To be fair, we are not sure, but there has been some issues as far back as when Kahlahnni was Branded. Evan was investigating, and handed the job onto Zussya when he left to protect Samarra, and when I returned from meeting the Seer and Captain, I promised I would aid Zussya in the continued search," Harlonngraith began his explanation.

Platisse nodded but looked doubtful. "And him?" He nodded his head toward Tom. "Why is he here? If you wanted it secret, why bring him in? He tried to take your throne not that long ago."

"I put Tommofey on the spot at the coronation and asked him what he would do first as king. His answer was to find out if there was a problem with the Branding ceremony. It was certainly a surprise."

Fabriolla the teal clothed Sister cleared her throat just as Platisse began to speak. Tom was grateful as it gave him a chance to count backwards from five to reign in his temper before he said something to his rude brother. "And I am assuming I am here because I have access to the records?" she spoke cheerfully.

Harlonngraith inclined his head at the rosy-cheeked, long-nosed woman. "Zussya claims you are the best re-searcher he knows and can be trusted above all others."

"I thought Shullamith was the best educated amongst us?" Platisse interjected, and it was all Tom could do to refrain from groaning at the whining man. Was this what Tommofey sounded like to others? No wonder Aviva used to get annoyed.

"Shullamith is an excellent educator and accomplished scholar, which is why I have placed you under him to study. Fabriolla, as she has stated, has access to the Tower of Records and has a memory like no other for recalling things she has read and is brilliant at making connections between information that others would never think of," explained Zussya.

It suddenly occurred to Tom to question why Platisse was even in the room. He held no expertise and hadn't been aware that there may be an issue. Was this Harlonngraith's way of forcing the three brothers to work together in the hope they forged some sort of bond? Tom had every intention of working with this group if it meant finding out why his beloved Aviva was Branded a Servant, but he had no intention of ever liking or becoming friends with his brothers.

Chapter 14

Samarra

Water lapping the side of the boat and whispered voices filled the cool damp night as Marra waited for the barge to be tied to the dock. She pulled the heavy cape tighter around her shoulders and looked over to the short woman beside her. Lahnni stood straight, her eyes scanning the shore, her legendary black feathered cloak glistened as the light from the bright torches were held aloft on the side of the bank. They both waved to Lopakka before concentrating on climbing onto the pier.

It was nearing midnight when they arrived at Ohanelle—the only Pomaikkan city in Segarris. This had been a deliberate decision by Kahlahnni, in the hope that it would keep the fanfare of her and Marra's arrival down to a more manageable event. She had explained to Marra that in the eyes of the Pomaikkan's, it was like Lahnni was returning home after being away for almost two decades, but to the Seer it was something she tried not to think about, as she didn't consider anywhere her home. Marra had hugged her and realized there was still so much about her mother's early life she didn't know. In some ways, Marra's childhood was based on lies, but now was not the time to unpack that. Instead, she comforted her mother and told her that if it helped, Marra thought of home as people not a place, and wherever her parents and Harley were was home to her.

With minimal fuss, their bags were transferred from the royal barge to the docks, where there were several carts waiting. Lopakka silently greeted them both with a firm, warm embrace. He was the first Pomaikkan that Lahnni had ever met, and was Marra's teacher when she had last visited and her Gift uncovered.

"Walk or cart?" he asked quietly.

"Walk," they answered in unison.

"Thought that would be the case. Being cooped up on a boat for all that time will make even the laziest want to stretch their legs when they get ashore."

The King's guards that had been sent with them formed around the women and Lopakka, allowing the carts to go ahead.

"Is this all necessary?" asked Lopakka.

"We will escort you to the gate and then I will hand over care to your people," the Captain of the guard answered curtly. "I assume there will be adequate measures taken to look after the safety of the Seer and the Queen?"

"Of course, though if I remember correctly, the Queen is also the Champion of our King?"

"Yes, but she is still recovering from her injuries at the Arena, and may I remind you the last time she was here she stopped an assassins attack? I do not believe I am asking too much for your cooperation in this?" The guard's look was challenging.

Marra felt the familiar pang of pain as she remembered her Bonding night and how she had fought assassins, with Harley, in the bathing rooms. She had lost a new-but-dear friend in Eltta. She wanted to argue that she was capable of taking care of any situation, but at this moment knew that wasn't true, no matter how much she wished it otherwise. It was her hope that by the time they left to return to the capital, Marra would be back to her full strength and fighting capabilities.

"How is your father?" Lahnni asked as they began to make their way through the small town that sat next to the walled settlement. The town was mostly merchants coming to barter their goods, or outsiders who had set up taverns and such for the said merchants to stay in while they did business. It was seldom that outsiders were allowed in the Settlement of the Roamers.

"Grumpy that you chose to arrive so late and that he can't come to greet you."

Lahnni laughed. "Nothing new about the grumpiness."

"True," agreed Lopakka. "I am certain he wouldn't know what to do if he didn't have something to complain about."

"You are both being mean," Marra interjected. "He was kind and sweet to me last time I was here."

"Are we talking about the same man?" joked his son.

"Yes," Marra said tartly, enjoying the banter. Everyone was so serious around her now; it was nice to be with someone who didn't appear fazed by all her titles.

"He was sweet and kind to me in the beginning too," amended Lahnni. "It wasn't until he got me back here and began to train me that the grumpiness showed itself."

They had arrived at the open gate that marked the entrance to Ohanelle. The carts could be heard off in the distance, rumbling their way to the women's sleeping quarters. The warriors that escorted them stopped and waited for further instruction.

"Thank you, Captain," Lahnni spoke. "When we are ready to leave, we will send word to the barracks."

"As soon as I see your escort I will hand over your safety to them. Until that time, we will remain here." The captain was clearly not going to budge on this.

Lopakka sighed dramatically and Marra hid a grin as she heard the soft whisper of fabric just before several Pomaikkan's materialized before them clad in dark clothing with weapons strapped to their backs.

"Good," was the only comment the captain said before ordering his men to fall back.

Marra looked at the eight assembled warriors and inwardly groaned; she hoped they were not going to follow her around everywhere.

"Those better be for mother," she grumbled.

This brought a smile to Lopakka's face. "No wonder you don't think Heiranni is grumpy; you sound just like him. Move along." He looked pointedly at the backs of the King's guard.

"Fine," she muttered and followed him through the gate and down the wide street.

They didn't speak again until they reached the large open square in the center of the city which was used for all major events as well as the daily market. The large open platform with its round wooden pillars stood in the center of the square, reminding Marra of the first time she had come to the Settlement and how that was the day her Gift as a Soul Sleeper had been revealed.

Four of the warriors bowed and disappeared into the night, leaving four.

"Two will remain with Kahlahnni at all times. I know it is a hindrance and unusual, but since the assassins were sent and no one knows from where or why we will be taking no risks with your life."

"Of course." Lahnni nodded. "Since my return, I have become accustomed to being guarded when Evannderth is not with me."

"And two will be with Lady Samarra until our head instructor tells me they are no longer needed."

Marra went to protest.

"Don't bother," Lopakka spoke firmly. "I accept that you could still defend yourself better than almost anyone, but there were three assassins last time and you are not up to that challenge. I will not be answering to your father or the King if something were to happen to you while you complete your training," he explained.

She wanted to complain, to shout that it was unfair, but instead, held her tongue and nodded because she knew she was out of sorts. Secretly, she was beginning to think that returning may have been a mistake. She loved Harley with all her heart, but things were complicated and expectations and responsibilities were being piled on quicker than she could adjust to. Now there was to be a royal wedding and a coronation, and if they were anything like the extravagance of the weddings she had seen on TV over the years, all the attention she would receive was more than a little daunting. On top of that, was the growing pressure to know more about her dreams and save them all before the perceived impending disaster struck.

"What, no arguments?" he joked.

"No, I am too tired to fight. Maybe tomorrow," she said tartly, which brought a chuckle from him. "What I do want to know is if you got my message about my dream?"

"Yes. We will join you in the morning and break fast together. Father and I are keen to hear everything but want you rested. It can all wait. Tonight you sleep."

I *wish*, Marra thought to herself. Sleep was something she had come to loathe.

Chapter 15

Samarra

The following day dawned bright and sunny and Marra felt disoriented as she woke. The last eight months had been a whirlwind of events and each morning it took her a moment to register just how life-changing her choices had been. While her friends had changed jobs, boyfriends, and haircuts, she had moved worlds, almost died, and was about to marry a king. It was a lot to take in, no matter how well-adjusted you were.

The small house they had been assigned was perfect. A two-bedroom with a kitchen, eating area, and a bathing room, with separate garderobe. The beds were large and soft with light blankets and fluffy feather-filled pillows. Everything was painted in a white wash and there were bold splashes of color in the abstract artwork and clutter.

Marra dressed quickly in her simple black ghi and she instantly felt like her old self. She efficiently braided her hair and washed her face before slipping out the door, trying not to wake her mother. Two guards followed her as she headed to the training area of the city. Marra chose not to let it get to her; instead, she focused on not getting turned around as she made her way through the slowly waking streets. It didn't take long for her to find the training areas, and she smiled to herself as she realized how her confidence had grown. A year ago, walking into a place by herself would have been scary, her shyness making it difficult, but now she had faced death and nothing seemed quite so terrifying. Though her shyness was still there with new people, her ability to deal with them had become better.

There were only two other people already slowly running through their katas, and neither bothered to look to see who had joined them. They were here for a purpose, not to be distracted. Though to be fair, they probably also assumed it was just one of the regulars who came this early as Marra stayed to the back of the open area.

It felt strange to start her warm-up routine and go through the paces of her first kata without the watchful eye of her friend Eltta in attendance. He had been the first person who had become a friend in her new home and he had died protecting her and Harlonngraith on their Bonding night.

Several more people joined the morning workout before one of them was alert enough to register Marra in their midst. She had to admit that she thought her taller stature and long blonde hair would have brought her recognition a little sooner.

"Lady Samarra, what a surprise," exclaimed a young woman as she walked into the area. Marra noted that the other five occupants, who were all spread out in front of her in the large space, turned quickly at the loud announcement of her name.

Ellei hurried over to Marra and moved to embrace her before remembering who stood in front of her and stopped just in time to drop into a deep curtsy.

"Save that for my mother." Marra laughed and reached out to embrace the short woman. "It is good to see you again, Ellei."

"The Seer is here?" There was a hint of awe to her voice.

"Yes. Mother and I are here for a visit."

By this time, the other five Pomaikkan's, who had been training, had come to gather around her. Several offered Marra their congratulations for her win in the Arena. She inclined her head in acknowledgment, but didn't want to talk about it.

"The King did not come with you this time?" one of the older men asked.

Marra shook her head. "No, he remained behind. He has much to see to and a wedding to organize."

"A wedding?" a mid-thirties woman asked.

"Yes, for me to be made Queen we have to be married in some form of church service."

"And you don't want to organize a big fancy wedding?" The young woman seemed shocked at Marra for not wanting to deal with all those minute decisions.

Marra fake shuddered. "Definitely not. I needed to come and complete my training before I took on the role as Queen, so it was a good excuse to leave it to others."

"I am sure your mother has it well in hand," the older man said.

"Oh, the Seer is here," announced Ellei, clearly enjoying the moment of knowing something no one else did.

"Kahlahnni has returned? Why were we not informed?"

Marra almost rolled her eyes at the man and his attitude. Why would he have been informed?

"We arrived last night," she explained instead. She looked over to her two guards and one nodded his head at her. "I am sorry, but I need to go. I only came down to stretch and run through a few katas. Perhaps I will see you again tomorrow?"

With a small apologetic wave to Ellei and a smile for the rest, Marra walked over to the guards and they fell in behind her as she made her way back to the small house. The streets now beginning to fill with people on early morning errands or off to work. Marra kept her head down and tried not to make eye contact to avoid being held up to talk to people. It was only now did she realize that she was not ready to answer people's curious-but-personal questions about her battle to the death as Harlonngraith's Champion.

As she reached the door to the house, it opened and Lopakka stood there. Marra turned to the two guards that followed her.

"There is no reason you can't train with me tomorrow morning, is there?" she asked. "If you must be here, at least make it useful. Yes?"

They didn't answer her, instead they looked to the middle-aged man in her doorway.

"That sounds like a perfectly acceptable compromise," he agreed. "Though, I will have to clear it with the man that is actually in charge of your safety."

"And who would that be?" she asked.

"Malekko, he is Eltta's replacement. Doesn't quite have his predecessors touch with the children, but is an exceptional teacher and fighter."

"Marra will help him in that area while she is here." Lahnni spoke over the shoulder of Lopakka. "She has always been wonderful with children."

"I will help where I can," Marra agreed. Lopakka stepped back into the house, allowing Marra to enter and close the door.

"Is she back?" grumbled a voice from the kitchen in the back of the house.

This made Marra grin and hurry to greet the old man.

"Heiranni." She rushed to his side and engulfed him in a hug. She was taller by a head and strong compared to the body frame she felt under his clothes. "You look well." Marra let him go and looked him up and down.

"You don't. Girl, are you sleeping at all? Has all your training gone out the window?" He looked at her pointedly.

"Be gentle, Teacher." Lahnni spoke quietly. "She has been through much."

"Bah, you coddle her." He dismissed her mother's words. "She is stronger than you think."

Kahlahnni looked to Marra then back at Heiranni. "She is brilliant, strong, and capable, but she is human and is healing from wounds you cannot see."

His glittering brown eyes wrinkled further as he glared at both the women. "Sit, and tell me what I am missing."

"I will get us breakfast." Marra went to move to the stove.

"No, Lopakka will do that. You will sit and tell me what I need to hear."

Marra sat at the small square table, but didn't say anything. Lahnni sat opposite her and smiled reassuringly—it didn't help. Marra did not return the smile.

"Kahlahnni, where have you been? Samarra would not tell us and kept repeating that if you wanted me to know you would tell me yourself." Heiranni's voice held a hint of exasperation.

Marra hid her relief at not being the one he had chosen to focus on first. The old man was intimidating at times and made her shyness assert itself. Lopakka did not have the same effect on her, fortunately she found him easy to be around when he was instructing her about her Gift.

"I have been farther than you would believe and it no longer matters as we won't be returning there. It served its purpose and kept me and Marra safe while she grew." Kahlahnni was circumspect in her answer.

"That's it? That's all I get?" Heiranni scowled at her.

"Yes."

"Fine." He turned his watery brown eyes towards Marra and she tried not to squirm in her seat. "You won the Right to Rule Challenge but were injured in the battle?" Heiranni asked, which Marra thought was odd, as Lopakka had clearly stated the night before that he knew she wasn't up to her usual fighting capacity, which meant he knew she was injured.

"Yes."

"Bad enough to halt your training?"

"Yes."

"How badly?"

"I almost died." Her voice was flat. She tried not to think about waking in the hospital connected to all the machines.

"But you did not." It was not a question, but rather a statement.

"She did not, but she should have," interjected Lahnni.

This made Heiranni turn from Marra and face the Seer.

Lopakka placed freshly cut fruit, with an assortment of nuts arranged on a star shaped platter on the table.

"What aren't you two telling us?" Lopakka asked as he settled into his seat and offered freshly brewed tea to them.

"Why are you pretending you don't know she was badly injured?" Lahnni countered.

Marra loved how her mother was such a straight talker. She tried to be like that, but it was only with her parents that she felt comfortable enough to express herself in that way. Harley was also becoming another she felt she could reveal herself completely to and speak her truth. It was taking time, but over the last nine months or so they had grown so close and she could see the depth of their respect and love continuing to grow.

"I was there," admitted Lopakka. "I saw her collapse, after killing the other Champion. I witnessed her wounds and none that I could see were life-threatening. But later, we received word from the Twin Cities that Samarra was gravely injured and no one would answer any further questions."

"Why did you not make yourself known?" asked Lahnni.

"It was only when you walked out into the Arena did I realize you had returned, by then it was too late to reach you. After the battle you were clearly distressed, and before I could get to you we were all removed by order of the King. I tried to find you later only to discover you were already moving, hurrying your daughter to the palace, which is when I became suspicious." Lopakka reached out and took several grapes and popped one in his mouth.

Marra smiled to herself as she realized he had deliberately stopped there in the hope of getting an answer without having to ask a question. The small kitchen filled with silence as he and her mother played their own game of chicken.

"Will you two ever grow up?" grumbled Heiranni. "Bah, they are like siblings," he complained to Marra. "Always playing games and trying to win at some stupid thing."

This made Lahnni laugh and Lopakka narrowed his eyes at her. "Fine. I became suspicious because if Samarra was that injured, why would you move her? And not just a short distance but weeks of travel. It made no sense."

"Marra went into the Challenge with injured ribs from the assassins attack."

All three adults gave Marra varying degrees of the same look and she concentrated on choosing a slice of apple rather than facing them

"I had no choice," she muttered. "He would have died if I didn't fight."

Lahnni chose not to reprimand her, instead she continued to answer Lopakka's question. "Shai, Tommofey's Champion, figured it out and continued to strike that area in the hope of weakening her. He managed to break her rib badly enough that one punctured her lung. Because she continued to fight rather than stop at that point the small puncture became a tear. We knew she was dying when she collapsed and that there was no hope in saving her." The Seer's voice was choked with emotion. "Harlonngraith ordered the Arena emptied so we could sit in vigil and allow our girl to pass in peace." Tears shone in Lahnni's eyes, and surprisingly, Heiranni reached out and patted her hand. The Seer went on. "At that time, a priest approached us and said he could help keep her alive if we agreed to not ask questions. We of course agreed instantly."

Lahnni sipped her tea, took a deep breath, and smiled at Marra, as if reminding herself that all was well and she could let the pain of that time go. Marra could only imagine what her parents and Harley had felt at that moment, being offered hope when seconds before there was none.

"He put her in some kind of stasis. Her breathing was so slow that we thought she had died anyway. His instructions were to not sit her up at any cost, she had to remain lying down. If she were sat up, her body would return to normal and her injuries would kill her. That was how we were able to get her to the capital to better healers and allow her body to rest."

Instead of the disbelief Marra expected from the men, they both wore an expression she couldn't place. What were they thinking? Why were they not bombarding Lahnni with questions?

"Now who is keeping secrets?" Kahlahnni looked pointedly at the two men.

"Ha, now you know what it feels like," Lopakka retorted.

He and Lahnni really did bicker like siblings.

It was amusing to witness, Marra thought.

"It's not that we are keeping secrets, it's rather that we are astounded at what you have revealed and are taking a few moments to digest it," Heiranni intervened. "Can you tell me anything about this priest? What order did he belong to?"

"He wore a black robe, had a beard and shaved head, so I assumed he was from the Order of Seggar."

"That's not a lot to go by. Name or anything?" Lopakka asked.

"I was preoccupied watching my daughter die, and when he gave me an ounce of hope, I didn't think to ask," Lahnni snapped. She took a steadying breath and went on, her voice a little less snarky. "It was only after we had begun the journey back to the Twin Cities did I try to look for the man to question him about what he had done. But he had disappeared, and Arch Deacon Zussya, who

I assumed was of the same Order, had no idea who I was referring to."

"I would like to find him and thank him when we get back," added Marra.

"And I will be joining you when you return to the palace," announced Lopakka. "I want to meet this man and study him if he allows me."

"Why?" asked Lahnni before Marra could.

"Because if I am right he is Gifted."

Lahnni nodded, but Marra was confused. "Hang on, what do you mean?"

"The priests that perform the Branding ceremony are supposedly Gifted in some way," she told Marra.

"It's a little more complicated than that, but I must admit to not knowing enough about it myself, which is why I want to talk to this man." Lopakka looked to his father, which made Lahnni and Marra also look at the old man.

Heiranni cleared his throat before answering the unspoken question. "The little I understand of the priests, for they keep their secrets, just as we do, the Branding ceremony is performed by priests who are able to channel with the will of the Gods. There seems to have been a changing of how things were done only a few decades after Segarris was united, but our records have several holes, even though we must participate like every other citizen in the Branding Ceremony in our nineteenth year. But as there are never any surprises, as we all end up with the Roamer Brand, there has never been much documentation. It is only the rare moments of the Gifted

Brand showing up that we researched and took note of in our records. Perhaps it was an oversight but not one we can go back and change."

"Okay, but why is this man different?" persisted Lahnni.

"It should be obvious. The priests are Gifted in their ability to Brand people, but I have never heard of anyone capable of more. He somehow stopped time, or slowed Marra's body enough to stop her from dying immediately."

Marra was only half listening. There was something going on in the back of her mind, like when you had an itch in the middle of your back but couldn't get to it. It was always just out of reach. "The priests with the Gifted Brand can mark the body, but he did more." She thought through her idea, speaking slowly. She frowned and struggled to find the words to what she was trying to uncover. Marra closed her eyes and began the process of settling herself, she had come to think of it as almost like putting herself in a trance. She no longer needed to always be fully asleep to replay a past dream if she was familiar enough with it.

She slowed her breathing and clenched her fists before letting them unfurl, but all she was met with was blackness. No dream, vision, or image. Just total darkness. What did it mean?

Chapter 16

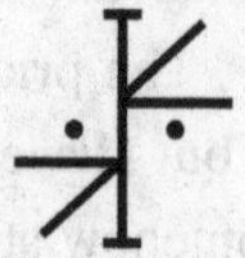

Tommofey

"Wait here," the King ordered his personal body-guard as he opened the door and stepped aside. A young page about the same age as Griggory went to walk in. "No, Arris, you wait here as well."

The boy and guard held their tongue but both looked at Tom and quickly averted their eyes. Clearly, they didn't trust him. Could he blame them?

"What do you think?" Harlonngraith asked as he escorted Tommofey into the newly refurbished room.

Tom still felt it odd every time his brother asked his opinion. He had spent his entire childhood and teen years being told that Harlonngraith was not to be trusted, that it was hard to reconcile the man that stood before him, to the monster his mother had painted. It was almost as if he was trying to be friends, but Tom was cautiously still waiting for the other shoe to drop. For why would the King want to be friends with the person that tried to take his crown? But the more optimistic side of Tom, the part that Aviva had showered with love and support, hoped that it was simply a brother trying to find a way to connect and move forward.

Tom looked around the room and was impressed by the transformation. "You would not think it was the same room," he commented.

Harley smiled broadly, like he was pleased with the simple praise. "Right?"

Tom moved further into the family library of his forefathers and took in the changes Harlonngraith had made. The large bookshelves that took up one entire wall still held many books, rolled scrolls, and several stacks of paper, but they were tidied and the shelves now painted white. The wide paneled wood floor had been sanded back and polished until it gleamed and now held several plush rugs in varying sizes and designs in the assigned seating areas, making each section feel cozy. The fireplace mantle had been rebuilt with dark blue marble with streaks of gold and appeared to set the color theme of the room. There was now a three seater couch facing the low burning fire in a heavy white material with square side tables that held an intricate lantern of gold on each. The darker blue rug was lush, and looked like something you would feel comfortable walking barefoot on and digging your toes into. Along the back of the lounge was a set of shelving also in white that housed woven baskets. It was a clever idea and something Tom had never seen before.

A rectangle table, in the same wood tone as the floor and baskets, had replaced the worn old desk and now sat in front of the second set of bookshelves on the wall opposite the fireplace. There were three chairs on each long side and one at each end. Though, Tom guessed you could add another four chairs easily, if required. The table was set up with several trays of food, a flagon of wine, a small barrel of mead, and gold mugs and goblets. There was a small stack of books, several quills, inkpots, blotters and blank parchment, ready for the coming meeting.

"Your decorator has excellent taste," Tommofey said as he stopped in the middle of the room. "Though, I am surprised at the darker blue."

"I created the design of the room and chose the colors, fabrics, and where to put everything." Harlonngraith spoke with pride. He looked around the room before meeting Tom's gaze. "The blue was father's color. Not as dark as yours, nor as light as mine, something in between. Perhaps a joining of both." Harley shrugged and looked away, out the large window. "And in all honesty, it matches the gold and white better than my sky blue."

Tom also looked toward the window and took in what he thought was the most welcoming part of the make-over. Sitting in front of the large pane of almost clear glass were two wide, high-backed chairs, each with its own matching footstool. They were velvet in the darker blue and had gold padded buttons in a double row on the back of the chair and brocade gold cushions in their corners. Tall gold candelabra sat on either side of the window frame, and another white, square side table sat between the chairs. The table held a small wooden tray that contained a single white leather bound book with the Gifted Brand embossed in gold on its cover, a gleaming gold ink pot and a matching gold quill with a thick black feather on its end.

"You have thought of everything."

"Not quite." Harlonngraith turned away from the window. "Did you not notice something was missing?"

Tom frowned and looked around the room. He had only been in here once before, for the brief meeting with his brother on his coronation day, and they had been joined by the Seer. It had been a difficult day and one he got through by sheer will at times. Tom finally noted the bare wall above the fireplace. There had been an impressive map that spanned that wall before. "The map is gone."

"Yes. Lady Samarra told me that you mentioned you were interested in cartography. I was going to have it restored and rehung but I thought perhaps you might be able to help me with something."

"I can try." Tom felt a sense of something other than sadness or anger for the first time since the Arena. It was odd and almost felt like a betrayal to the memory of Aviva and Shai.

"I will have the map restored and rehung, but I am having a copy made and would like for you to look at it and add anything that you know of that is missing. Is that something you could do? I am uncertain as to your expertise in the area." Harlonngraith blew out his breath and walked over to the table. "Wine?" he asked as he reached for the flagon.

"Is it red?" Tom found himself asking.

"Yes, I enjoy a red wine, though I rarely drink."

It surprised the prince to find another thing in common with his brother. Tommofey watched in amazement as his brother, the King of Segarris, didn't call a servant, but instead poured them both a goblet of the blood red wine. "You honor me."

Harlonngraith looked surprised. "I do? How?"

"You trust me enough to have no guard in here with us, and now you pour me a beverage with your own hands."

This made Harlonngraith laugh. "But do you trust me enough to drink what I pour you?"

Tom laughed nervously. Did he trust him enough? Did it matter? "I don't think you gave me my life to only snuff it out with poisoned wine."

"Mmm...maybe." Harlonngraith held out the goblet while he took a sip of his own. His gray eyes gave away nothing.

Without hesitation, Tom took the proffered cup and brought it immediately to his lips, the pain he felt most days was never ending, and if the wine was going to kill him his only hope was for it to be quick. He downed the whole glass and held it out for a refill.

"Well played." Harlonngraith smiled and took the goblet. "What do you think about helping me with the map? Would you care to take a look?"

Tom blinked. This man was all over the place. "I would be happy to take a look, but can't promise anything. I did take notes while I was traveling, perhaps I could add something to that area."

"All I will ever ask is for you to do your best." Harlonngraith handed him the refilled cup. "Between you and me, I think our mothers and father didn't do a great job at ruling. There seems to be quite a few things fallen by the wayside in favor of frivolous pursuits and father continuing going off to fight skirmishes that he didn't need to. I have so many things on my plate, and with a wedding on top of it, I fear my mind is bursting. I am trying to learn to trust and delegate, but it is hard when my mother has raised me to trust no one but myself."

"Oh, I do understand that. It seems we have more in common than I first thought. Trust is something I also find difficult." Tom thought about the slowly developing friendship he had with Pynnan and Albertinne. He liked them, but did he trust them? Was it his upbringing or was it more?

Harlonngraith put down his goblet and held out his hand. Tom looked at it for a moment before he did the same. They grasped each other's forearms. "I promise no more threats of poisoning your wine."

Tom laughed. He was coming to enjoy his brother's sense of humor. "I would appreciate it. And I promise not to try to overthrow you again."

Harlonngraith joined in the laughter. "I think the whole country, aside from your mother, would appreciate that."

"I can't disagree on that one," Tom answered with a straight face.

This brought on howls of laughter and a fair bit of back slapping. They were interrupted when the door was opened and Platisse and Zussya entered the room. Both priests looked shocked at what they found. The Arch Deacon's round, bearded face moved from shock to pleased quickly, but Tom noted that his other half-brother Platisse didn't have the same reaction. There was loathing and suspicion before it was replaced by a pleasant half smile, that was fake to anyone with eyes. Tom straightened and took up his goblet, settling his face into the same half pleasant smile, but he was better at hiding his dislike. There was something about these two that made him wary.

Though Arch Deacon Zussya had never given him any reason to not trust him, he just didn't. It could possibly be that even though this was the fifth time they had met regarding trying to discover any issues with the Branding ceremonies, both priests from the Order of Seggar were not adding anything of value in Tom's opinion. He wasn't sure they were being entirely honest about the entire situation. And even though she was touted as having amazing research skills, Fabriolla had also contributed little to the research so far. He was beginning to believe the church was hiding something.

Chapter 17

Samarra

Samarra pulled her punch inches before it connected to her sparring partner, and while it still made him stagger back and exhale loudly, it didn't knock him on his arse like she wanted to. Malekko, Eltta's replacement, was an exceptional fighter and teacher, just as Heiranni had claimed, but he was not interested in learning anything from Marra when it came to handling children. After another unsuccessful attempt at trying to help with the littles that wanted to learn martial arts, and Ellei had confided to Marra that there had been an influx of young girls since Marra's victory at the Arena, Marra had left to train on her own and blow off some steam.

Malekko had found her a half turning later helping a few adults with their technique and commented that perhaps she would like to spar with him as a final test to make certain she had recovered fully from her injuries. Without a second thought, Marra had accepted.

Nothing had gone to plan since she had returned to Segarris, and Marra was out of sorts, and she was now taking her bad mood out on the arrogant instructor. She allowed him to regain his footing and breath before she launched another series of blows, this time combining it with a sweeping kick. He blocked all her strikes and avoided her kick and she nodded once in acknowledgment of the feat. Her body felt good. She had lost a little of her speed and strength, but now she was fully healed, that would come back quickly when she returned to training properly. To beat Malekko, Marra was relying on muscle memory, her superior skill set, thanks to her father, and a brewing resentment.

Malekko advanced with a flurry of strikes aimed at her head and chest, but as he went on, the mood changed. She felt it shift and she knew from the way he was making her lift her arms to defend herself that he was about to try and hit her in her ribs. Her anger roiled and the pent up frustration at her inability to find equilibrium in her life with her Gift rose up. The swing came and her survival instinct to protect the damaged area took over.

A loud crack resounded around the sparring area as Marra broke Malekko's arm.

Samarra hung her head as she waited for the punishment that would soon be meted out by the group of Pomaikkan men and women who sat at the table upon the platform in the center of the community square. Regardless of her titles, she would accept her punishment like any other citizen. Marra was embarrassed by her lack of control and the pain she had caused Malekko. When would she learn to control her temper? She thought she had mastered it in the Arena, but it appeared otherwise.

"Bah," said Heiranni, and he dismissed the entire situation with one word. This brought Marra's head up. "The fool is lucky you didn't kill him for trying to take that cheap shot. I have been informed that he has not taken heed of my suggestion to have you help train the young ones. So, I say your punishment will be to take over all of his training commitments for the next six weeks while his arm heals."

There were several nods from others at the table. "Agreed," even more announced loudly.

They looked to Marra expectantly and she suddenly understood that they were hoping she would go along with the judgment. Marra could just pack up and leave, or simply say no, after all she was Bonded to the King, and a Soul Sleeper, but she did neither. Instead, she raised her voice so all those gathered could hear. "I accept the responsibility of taking on the instructors' classes for the next six weeks."

"Good, it's done. Now everyone go about your day," an old woman announced in a loud voice.

Marra waited at the edge of the platform with Lahnni. Many people looked like they wanted to approach the two of them but held back out of respect. "Bah, off with the lot of you," growled Heiranni as he moved to the top step.

Marra smiled up at him and held out her hand—being taller than everyone had its advantages. She was easily able to offer him assistance with the stairs. He waved her hand away.

"Don't be a fool," admonished Kahlahnni. "The Soul Sleeper is offering you her hand as reconciliation." She paused for a moment. "Or at least that's what everyone else will believe. You should be using your stick."

"I don't need a lecture from you; I get enough of those from my son." But he took Marra's hand and held it tightly as he moved down the few steps.

"Where is your son?" asked Lahnni. "I thought he would be here? What was so important he had to miss it?"

Marra rolled her eyes at the barb and tried not to smirk. Her mother never behaved like this with anyone else. The rivalry between the two was growing daily and Marra was there for it. It was the only thing that kept her thoughts away from her own misery.

"Why don't you go find where Lopakka is and stop pestering me with silly questions," Heiranni answered. "Leave Samarra with me. She can make sure I get home safe as I am so decrepit," he finished sarcastically.

This made Marra laugh openly, and it was a small relief after the build up of the morning.

"Yes, I just might do that," said Lahnni

"Orrrr," Heiranni said, drawing out the word. "You might consider sitting up on the step and allowing a few people to approach you. You have kept to yourself since your return to Ohanelle and I am certain there are people who would like to say hello after all this time. You have the guards to keep you safe if there is an issue."

Kahlahnni looked to the small group of people that had not returned to their duties now the meeting was over. They were clearly waiting for either the Seer or the Soul Sleeper or both. She looked to her daughter.

"Yes, I will stay. You have been brave and heading out to be gawked at as the Soul Sleeper and Champion while I have hidden. It is time the Seer served more than the King."

Before Marra could do more than smile, Heiranni spoke. "Good. But don't overdo it on your first day back on the job." He turned to Marra. "Let's go."

As they walked away, the old man holding onto her arm like she was escorting him somewhere rather than for support, Marra managed to get Ellei's attention. The woman hurried over. "Mother is going to stay and chat for a while. I am certain the news will spread quickly. Get more guards and see that she has refreshments, please."

"Of course, Lady Samarra." Ellei hurried away, and Marra continued walking with Heiranni.

"You are a natural, you know," he commented as they took a turn down a smaller street, but with larger houses.

Marra looked down at him and raised her eyebrows. "At what?"

"You don't even think about it. You have your father's ability to see what is required and simply order it done. No fuss, no bother. Your mother can be a little more dramatic."

This made Marra chuckle. "Um, I think I am dramatic enough."

"Bah."

"I broke a man's arm for trying to punch me in the ribs," she pointed out.

This brought a small cackle from the old man. "Point taken."

They walked in silence until the end of the street. It ended in a large house with a beautiful garden out the front that held a huge lemon tree. A path split in two and led around the tree trunk on both sides, joining up on the other side and heading toward the brightly painted yellow door.

"Home," announced Heiranni proudly, as if Marra had never seen it before. "You will come next week for dinner?"

"Yes, I would like that," Marra agreed.

"Good. But now we talk. Come, sit." He led her to a bench that reminded her of the one in the family grove in Melbourne. This one sat under a large window, with a hedge full of white flowers behind it.

As she settled onto the stone bench, he didn't mince words. "Something is blocking you. Until you understand it, you will struggle to control your sleep and not get the rest you require. Having this ability is not easy, but I doubt it was also never supposed to be so hard that if you don't learn to control it you will go mad."

Marra knew he was right, but she didn't know what to do about it. Nothing worked. Being away from Harlonngraith and him not being there to sing her to sleep was making it worse.

As if reading her mind, Heiranni went on. "You can't rely on other people to comfort and ease you. Your mother found a man who didn't project his feelings and you found one willing to lose sleep every night to ease your nightmares, but you, like Lahnni had to do, must learn to do everything for yourself."

"Must you always compare me to my mother?" she asked with more hardness than she had intended. "Can't I just be me? I am Gifted like my mother, I am the Champion because of my father, I am now to be Queen to Harlonngraith. So many titles and none that I asked for." Her voice was weary. She was tired. So tired.

"You resent your parents for putting you on this path." Heiranni spoke. It was not a question.

Marra shrugged. "I feel like I have no free will." She looked down at the tattoos on her wrists. "I may not have been Branded like the rest of Segarris but I am still a pawn." She felt her frustration at the situation she found herself in growing as she spoke. As the words trailed away, Marra began to see how absolutely unreasonable her emotions were—after all weren't they all pawns? She tried to explain, and wished she could speak in English rather than Segarrin. Many words were similar, but there were still differences. "Look at mother who doesn't know how she ended up in Gennestmont in a boarding house for orphans. Or father, all set to be a noble and inherit titles and land and he ended up with a Warrior Brand. What if there was no Branding and they chose their own path?"

"Okay, let's play the what if," Heiranni said, his voice softer than usual. "What if your mother ignored everything and never sent the note on where Harlonngraith could find his Champion?" He didn't look at her; instead, he watched the lemon tree branches sway gently in the breeze. "Or go back further. What if you were never trained by your father? What if he ignored your mother's warning and didn't teach you everything he could? How far back do you want to go?

"What do you mean?"

"Exactly what I said. How far back do you want to go? What happens if your parents never left here to protect you and your mother? What happens if your father never rescued your mother from Darria? Or helped her find me to train her? You could play the what if game forever but it changes nothing." He stopped and turned on the bench to face her. His brown eyes not blinking. "Choices were made that the Gods had nothing to do with. Yes, they gave us Brands, and in your case, something even more unique, but it is what we do with them that makes us who we are. If you sat in a room and did nothing with your Gift and never got training and it eventually sent you mad because you could never rest, is that the fault of the Gods or you?

'Your parents made their decisions based on what they thought was best. They are good people who raised a kind, caring and remarkable woman, but without their choices you wouldn't be you. Now you make your own choices and your choice was to return here and take up the mantle of Soul Sleeper and Queen. How is either of those decisions anyone's fault?"

He made it seem simple, so easy to accept, but it ran-kled and she fought against the invisible yoke she now found placed around her neck. "I will keep working on it," she promised.

Marra stood there holding one shoe in her hand and immediately recognized the beginning of her dream. But this time, rather than experience it first-hand, she attempted something different. After the discussion with Heiranni about choices and being a pawn in someone else's game, Marra had been thinking about the things she could and could not control. She couldn't stop the dreams, no matter how she wanted to, so she made her choice to take control of them. Marra made a conscious decision within her dream, and something like the sound of a click echoed, and she floated backward, away from her body. No longer experiencing everything firsthand, she floated a little further back to see if she could get a better view and found herself being able to take in the scene as it unfolded.

Samarra watched herself search for her shoe, the other one held tightly in her grip. She noted the assassins' shadows standing in the corner waiting. The flashing of the Brands on the wall as they went through their cycle. Marra took it all in before she followed herself through the door, still in search of the answer but knowing it would not be in the next room. It never was. Instead, there would be the dais and the broken crown and the shadowed figure in the dark cloak holding the ring with the skeleton keys. Marra took in every detail, hoping to see something more. She took note that there were three keys. She didn't know if it was significant, but everything she dreamed could have a meaning or warning. The fleet of boats with their red flags snapping in the breeze appeared behind the throne, and she refused to look down and see the bodies of Harley and Tommofey slaughtered upon the dais.

The dream started again, and rather than fight it, Marra went with it, watching and hoping that something would stand out and give her a clue to what she was supposed to do with all the information. How many details had she missed because she was scared, tired, or too stubborn? As the dream repeated, Marra moved to a different position to try and get a new perspective. It wasn't until the fourth time the dream cycled did she realize that something was off with the placement of the bodies on the dais.

Marra had been avoiding looking at the dead body of her Bonded, but out of the corner of her eye, something had caught her attention. Before she had the chance to react further, the dream reset. Rather than fight it, she went through it again, but this time she didn't look at the things that always drew her attention, she looked at other things. Instead of the shoe she was carrying and the other she was searching for, what was she actually wearing on her feet?

The red roses she now knew represented death. That had been meted out several times now, plus the dead bodies on the dais confirmed that death might be coming.

Marra counted the symbols as they flashed through their sequence, all eight appeared. She counted the figures that stood along the wall in the shadows and took note of the type of door she walked through to go into the next room.

The moment had come and she floated closer as the dead bodies of the King and his brother materialized on the dais before the throne. Marra gasped as she realized that the bodies were too short for the six foot five Harlonngraith, and six foot seven Tommofey. They were shorter, closer to her own six-foot height. It was then that she noticed the ultra long blonde hair. "No," she said aloud in her dream. But knowing in the pit of her stomach that who she thought it was was correct. Marra could guess who the second body was.

Before her lay the two former Queens of King Tommofey. Slain in place of their sons. A fluttering of something caught her eye and the robed person behind the throne tossed his skeleton keys in the air and threw off his robe to reveal a shadowed figure of a man, but upon his forehead, over his heart, and on his stomach glowed the Brand of the Gifted.

The dream faded to only begin again. It was time to wake up. There were too many new things to take note of. She needed to talk it through with her mother, Lopakka, and Heiranni.

Marra woke to a pounding head and a look of concern on her mother's face hovering over her. She felt exhausted instead of rested.

"How long?" she asked, her voice rough from her dry throat.

"More than half the day. I was worried when you didn't come down for breakfast. Lunch was almost an hour ago."

"Turning," corrected Marra.

Lahnni made a sour face. "Yes, turning. I admire how quickly you have adapted." She stood and stretched her hands over her head. "I will get you a drink and something to eat."

"Thank you, but first send for Lopakka and Heiranni. I will bathe quickly and get changed and meet you all downstairs."

"Fine, but take your time getting up. You will be dizzy."

Rather than get upset or cranky at the over-mothering, Marra smiled at Lahnni. "Yes, I will be careful."

Lahnni left the room and Marra lay there for a little while longer before she pushed herself up to a sitting position. She swung her legs over the side of the bed and welcomed the cool wood floor on her bare feet. Her head felt heavy and cloudy, and Marra felt like she hadn't slept in a week. Slowly she stood and made her way to the bathroom she shared with her mother, and filled the basin with the water that sat in a pitcher on the windowsill. The heat of the sun had taken the biting chill off the water but it was still refreshing as she splashed it on her face.

Marra didn't have time to heat water over the fire and make a bath—god, she missed the ease of a shower—so she did a rudimentary wash with a cloth and changed into a ghi. She tied up her hair in her customary messy bun and slipped on her shoes. After telling the three adults her dream, she planned on heading to the sparring area and making good on her promise to train those that Malekko normally would.

With her head still pounding and hoping it was from dehydration and not something worse, Marra headed downstairs. Lahnni was just sliding a pile of scrambled eggs onto a plate as Marra sat at the table. Gratefully, she took a sip of the freshly squeezed juice and *ahhhed* as it slid down her parched throat. "Thank you," Marra said as she picked up her fork and took her first bite of the golden pile of yumminess.

There was a polite knock on the door and Lahnni called out, "Come in." She quickly washed up the few dishes she had used to make Marra's breakfast and sat them on a wooden drainer to dry.

"What's up?" Lopakka asked as slid into the chair next to Marra. "They look tasty." He eyed the eggs on her plate.

"Would you like me to make you some?" asked Lahnni.

Lopakka feigned shock. "Yes, please."

Lahnni smiled at him. "No time for sass today. Maybe later."

"If you two aren't going to bicker there must be a problem. Let's hear it," Heiranni announced as he poured himself a juice.

Between mouthfuls Marra quietly explained that she had had a breakthrough with her dreaming. That somehow she had managed to separate herself while Soul Sleeping. She went on to tell them how the bodies of Harlonngraith and Tommofey had become Anzhellika and

Darria, and that the figure that held the skeleton keys had thrown off his cape to reveal the glowing Brands on his forehead, heart, and stomach.

Lopakka clicked his fingers.

"Of course!" he said with excitement. "The three of you make the Ternion."

"The what?" asked Lahnni, setting down his plate of eggs. "Are you deranged?"

"No, no. Samarra said something a few weeks ago, when you arrived, and it's been playing over in my mind."

"What did I say?"

"You said the priests with the Gifted Brand can mark a body but it seems this priest can do more. You implied that there was more to say but you couldn't find the words."

"Yes, I remember. It was like an itch in the center of my back I couldn't quite get to. The answer was there, but I couldn't reach it."

Lopakka looked to Kahlahnni. "You are the Seer, you represent the heart, the desires of others." He turned to Samarra. "You are the Soul Sleeper, the Brand on the forehead is you. You interpret the things put into your head via your dreams." Lopakka looked to his father who was nodding his understanding or agreement, Marra wasn't sure. "And this priest could be the third piece to the Ternion."

"Yes, he has control over the body, which would match the Brand that was on his stomach." Lahnni said. "He touched Marra on her stomach when he put her in stasis."

"But what is a Ternion?" asked Marra.

Heiranni answered. "It's the combining of all three powers to create another power."

"And what is the other power?" persisted Marra—sometimes their half answered questions made her want to scream.

"We are not sure. There is mention of a Ternion, but not a description of what it does."

"Helpful," muttered Lahnni.

"There have been so few Gifts for centuries that the people who kept the records prior to our family taking over became lacks in creating copies of valuable tomes when the ink began to fade and become unreadable. Much of what we know now only comes from legends passed down and the bits and pieces we can cobble together as we try to save what we can."

Marra finished her food and took the last gulp of her juice. She knew the three of them well enough that they would sit here for several turnings rehashing what she had just told them and what it could all mean. This worked well for them, but lately Marra had discovered she did better when she moved and kept her mind busy rather than focusing all her attention on the problem. Her mind would continue to work on the issue in the background if she gave it enough time. And in a rather blasé fashion, she also knew that tonight she would more than likely have to experience the dream over and over, which made her want to avoid discussions for the sake of discussions about it.

"Where are you going?" asked Heiranni as Marra stood ready to leave.

"To fulfill my promise until I leave. I won't be able to stay the final three weeks. I will give you a week and run as many training sessions as I can for all those that still want to come to one."

"You made a promise," Heiranni stated bluntly.

"Yes, I did, but this takes precedent. You can live without my training. I need to get back and find the priest who carries the Gifted Brand and discover what I can about this thing Lopakka called the Ternion. We can send missives to Dad and Harlonngraith all we want, but Mum and I need to be there. We are too far away if something changes in our visions and dreams."

Chapter 18

Samarra

The fire crackled pleasantly as Marra sat in what was soon becoming her favorite place in the palace and watched the sun slide behind a few fluffy white clouds, like the ones you find in children's picture books. She loved the renovated family library and the large blue upholstered chairs with their footstools facing each other and angled to look out onto the city. Marra escaped to the room as often as she could to write and read and take a breath. It was a shame Harley could not be with her—they were struggling to find time together to connect and enjoy each other's company other than at night when they were both exhausted and sometimes overwhelmed with their new roles. Marra found the fact she couldn't go anywhere without at least two people following her to be quite disconcerting. She still struggled with many of the restricting aspects of royal life, if she was honest.

She was sleeping slightly better now Harley was near and singing her to sleep. But she would never find herself as well rested as she wished. Her brain fog was not clearing and she struggled with her dreams. The block

Heiranni had spoken of was still present—she could feel it in her dreams. Something was not right, even though she was more accepting of her situation and titles, but she had no idea how to fix it.

Life at the palace was complicated as she tried to learn her role. Anzhellika was always making it more difficult than it had to be, and Marra had found she was missing her friends more and more. She had no one to confide in. Though she felt she could talk to her mother and father and of course Harley, there was something she was missing. But how could she make friends when she was never around people? She amended that thought. Around people who weren't servants, or nobles still too anxious around her and her too many titles. The few nobles that did approach her and appear friendly, she felt that there was an underlying motive and it typically turned out that they wanted something from her. Which now made her more wary and isolated. Harlonngraith was so caught up in his own steep learning curve that she felt she couldn't rely on him more than she did, as he was already carrying so much.

A polite knock on the door was followed with it being opened by Arris, Harlonngraith's current Page. "I am to let you know that you have a visitor and the King requests you to come with me."

Marra didn't hesitate.

"Sure thing," she said cheerfully as she stood and maneuvered around the low table in the overly large hooped skirt she was now forced to wear on a regular basis. She was still trying to figure out if she could get away with wearing her ghi all the time, as it was the closest thing she had to loose comfortable clothing that she needn't worry about knocking something over with. Or perhaps she could modify a soldiers uniform as she did carry the Warrior Brand?

She followed Arris down the corridor, with her two personal bodyguards trailing behind her. They turned down several hallways, and crossed through the throne room, which currently stood empty, and made their way down another two corridors before they came to a group of people standing around. She identified them quickly. Two were Harlonngraith's personal guards, and they seemed to be blocking the doorway, as the door was opened upon her approach it looked to be a narrow corridor on the other side. Another two were the soldiers assigned to guard her mother, and the final pair of people were her father's aid and assigned page. He had refused guards and no one saw fit to argue with him.

"Your Highness, no one is allowed passed this point bar you," Arris informed her.

Everyone moved out of the way. As she passed by one of Harley's guards he spoke. "Fourth door on the right, Lady Samarra."

"Thank you." She walked through and the door was closed quickly behind her, leaving her in the semi-darkness of the narrow hallway. There was a small, thin window at the end of the corridor that let in weak sunlight. She guessed they were on the opposite side of the palace she had been sitting on only a quarter turning ago.

Before she had reached the first door, the fourth on the right opened and Harley stuck his head out. "Ah, there you are." He grinned and stepped out of the room, closing the door firmly behind him. He met her halfway up the corridor and smiled wickedly, lifting an eyebrow at her as he gently pushed her up against the wall. "Alone at last," he whispered as he brought his lips down on hers.

The soft kiss quickly turned passionate as his tongue sort hers. Marra reached up and ran her fingers through his light brown hair, while her other hand snaked under his jacket in an attempt to get to his skin. She moaned in the back of her throat. Half from desire and half from being thwarted by his shirt.

Harley pulled back slightly and kissed under her ear, sending a shiver down her spine. "One day I am just going to drag you into a room and have my way with you," he whispered, before kissing her there again.

"Why not now?" she breathed.

"Because your mother and father wait for us with someone you have been trying to find, and I have no desire to explain to them why I took so long to bring you in here." He let her go and stepped back into the center of the corridor.

Marra took a deep breath and pushed herself off the wall. Her insides were hot and bothered and it took all her control to not say screw it and drag him into the closest room just as he had suggested.

"Fine, but you owe me." Marra playfully glared at him as she smoothed her ridiculous skirts. After she was crowned Queen, Marra silently vowed to begin her campaign to change what was acceptable for her to wear. How was she ever supposed to defend herself in this get-up?

It was only as Harley opened the door for her did Marra stop to consider why all the secrecy to who she was meeting. In the small, bare room stood her father, mother and a man in a black priest robe. He had a shaved head and full beard that was mostly gray with matching bushy eyebrows. He was taller than her mother but shorter than her father, Marra guessed about five foot ten inches tall, and had a thin frame and face. His skin was dark, a deep rich brown, and his eyes were a startling bright hazel. He bowed deeply as she stopped in front of him.

"Lady Samarra, it is wonderful to see you well and healed." His voice was gentle and warm.

Her shyness took over and she smiled nervously and looked to her mother for some indication of what was going on.

"This is Brother Ahttoh." Evan was the one to answer. "He is the one who saved you."

"How did you find him?" she asked, looking at the priest and trying to figure out how she felt. Her father had been searching for him secretly since their return.

"He found me. I was waiting for one of my men in a local tavern when Brother Ahttoh came in and sat down."

Marra raised her eyebrows. "That seems a little too easy."

"My, you are a suspicious one," Ahttoh commented. "As I explained to your father, who just for the record was even more direct than you, I did what I could for you in the Arena, but trailed behind with the rest of the people returning to the Twin Cities in case I was needed. There was no word for a long time about your recovery so I went back to my job on the other side of the river, but kept waiting to discover what had happened to you. Then word spread that you had recovered and would be in attendance at the coronation. You were gone again so swiftly after that that when I had heard you had returned for the wedding I set about trying to find a way to meet you only to be told that Evannderth was looking for me. Something is happening and I can't explain it." His hazel eyes showed his confusion.

"Try," Marra suggested, her voice soft.

"It's like I needed to see you to be sure you survived. I have no idea why I feel this compunction."

Marra nodded, as if she understood, though she didn't. Her shyness was slowly fading. "And how do you feel now that you have seen me?"

"Relief that you live, but the pull is still there." Ahttoh paused then looked to Kahlahnni. "But what I thought was a pull towards the Lady Samarra seems to actually be divided between the both of you. Any idea why?" He frowned. "To be honest, it's a little disconcerting."

"We might have some idea, but first we need a few questions answered honestly." The Seer looked around the room. "Evannderth, would you be a dear and get some chairs? This could take a while."

"Is there a reason why we need to keep this meeting secret?" asked Harlonngraith. "We could always take this to a more comfortable location."

"For the moment, secrecy is best. Brother Ahttoh here is more than he seems and we still don't know who our enemies are. Let us not put him under any scrutiny," Lahnni explained. "Though a room with chairs and a drink would be nice."

"We can do that," Harley announced. "Follow me, please." He opened the door and they filed out into the corridor. They walked one door down and on the opposite side. Harley opened that door and stepped aside. "Go in, I'll be back in a moment."

Marra followed everyone in and closed the door. The room was slightly larger, with a table and chairs for six. There was a sideboard and a fireplace prepared and just waiting to be lit. Several slit-like windows with heavy drapes gave off the only light source and Evannderth quickly struck the flint sitting on the mantle to start the fire and took a lit twig and held it to the wick of the three squat yellow candles that sat upon the table. By the time they had settled into their chairs, the fire was burning brightly and Harlonngraith had returned announcing that refreshments were on their way. Arris would bring them down the corridor and knock then leave.

This all gave Marra time to watch Ahttoh and come to her own conclusions. Yes, she was still suspicious. It all seemed so easy. Her father had been looking for him and there Ahttoh was, but on the other hand, why did everything have to be difficult? Had there not been enough difficulty? And the compulsion he mentioned? She had to admit that when she sat still and watched him she felt it too, like a tenuous hand reaching out from her to him and her mother. She recognized that it had always been there with her mother, but had always thought it was just a special bond they shared, now Marra wasn't so sure. There was also something else she felt toward him and she acted on that now.

Marra reached across the table and took the older man's hand. He didn't pull back, but instead held her gaze.

"Thank you, for saving me. I am sorry I didn't say it as soon as I saw you. I should have."

"You are welcome. It was a risk to expose myself in that way, but you needed to live."

"Why?" asked Lahnni. "Why did she need to live?"

"I don't know. I wasn't even supposed to be there."

"You weren't?"

"No, I am too important to be wandering around doing my own thing. But I knew I needed to be there. I lied and told the tower I had a sick relative I wanted to visit and they allowed me a month off. People generously allowed me to travel with them as we all made our way to the Arena." He looked down at his cassock and the stole around his neck that indicated his rank in the church. "This certainly helped."

"I don't mean to appear rude, but what do you mean by you are too important?" Harlonngraith asked. "I thought I had met all the important clergy who lived in the Twin Cities."

"He is secret important," Marra said as she let go of his hand and sat back in her chair. "He carries the Brand of the Gifted."

"He's what?" asked Evannderth, showing his surprise for once.

"Lopakka suggested that to be able to do what he did, Ahttoh is possibly part of the secret group of priests that not only wear the Religious Brand but also the Gifted Brand. Much like you with your two Brands," Lahnni answered Evan.

They all looked expectantly at Ahttoh. The man took a deep breath as if about to explain everything when there was a loud knocking on the door.

"It's me with the food," announced Arris, his voice breaking halfway through the sentence.

Everyone remained silent as Harlonngraith waited by the door for several moments, giving the boy enough time to leave the hallway. He opened the door and picked up the covered tray and brought it into the room, before returning to collect the second tray, this one filled with goblets for six and two ewers.

"Six?" remarked Evan as he poured five drinks.

"Just in case someone was gossiping, better to throw them off what they think they know," explained Harley.

Evan gave him a nod. "Good, you learn quickly."

"You were about to explain your Brands," Lahnni brought the conversation back to Ahttoh.

"Yes, of course." The priest settled into his chair, cradling the goblet of cider in his hands. "You are correct. I do carry the Religious Brand on my left wrist, but also the Gifted Brand on my hip. A long time ago, those Branded in this way had the power to carry out the Branding Ceremony without using a Branding iron. But over time there was blame and unrest and accusations of priests misusing it or taking bribes to give people a different Brand than what they should have. It is difficult to do, but our will is supposed to be a conduit for the Gods and we see what the Supplicant is supposed to be, but on many occasions we can override it.

"King Russlonngraith," he looked to Harlonngraith, "one of your ancestors, ordered the Branding priests to find another way to continue Branding the castes without the interference of human choice. This, of course, they discovered was not possible but they did find a way to control it better. They brought all Gifted Priest's into the tower here in Arsenny that is the home of the Order of Seggar, and had them turn their abilities into infusing special rods of precious metal with a flat disc at its head. They then created a powder that activated the power when heated and anyone with the priest Brand was able to channel with the will of the Gods and Brand the citizens correctly. Those priests were not Gifted so could not control the outcome of the Branding Rod."

Ahttoh paused and took a sip of his cider. "I have been doing my own research for years as I noticed a sharp decline in the amount of priests who were being Branded with the double Brand. There were never more than ten at any time, but also no fewer than six."

"How many are there now?" asked Evan.

"Three. Which is even worse if you consider that our population is growing. With the joining of the separate countries, which are now the Provinces of Segarris, we are stronger, more powerful, and other nations no longer invade us on a whim seeking our riches aside from the troubles in Lobbregath, which means our citizens don't die in needless war in the numbers they used to and are thriving and having babies."

"That makes absolutely no sense," Harlonngraith remarked.

"I assure you it is true. And with a larger population, you would think the Gods would provide us with more Gifted Priests not less," Ahttoh explained patiently.

"I am sorry, that was not what I was implying. With less chance of war, why has there been a massive surge in Warrior Brands?"

"There has?" Ahttoh seemed surprised. "No one has ever mentioned that to me. I have been focused on Gifted Priests and must admit not taking note of the overall population Branding. Obviously an oversight that needs to be rectified on my behalf."

"That seems to be a common occurrence," remarked Marra.

"Lopakka was remarking that they had not been looking at a bigger picture either, but rather focused on their little section of the Branding Ceremony."

"Will I get to meet this Lopakka, perhaps we can work together?"

"There is nothing that I could do to keep him away from you once he finds out we have met," admitted Marra.

"I think we should also introduce Fabriolla to you. The three of you may be able to work better together rather than the group I have currently working on the oddities of the Branding Ceremony. Platisse and Tommofey seem to rub each other the wrong way continually, and Platisse is at times openly hostile, which is making everyone uncomfortable. Zussya seems somewhat preoccupied and honestly not much is getting done," Harlonngraith explained. He turned to Evan for confirmation.

"Yes, I agree. Perhaps we should adjourn the weekly gatherings on the pretext of allowing them to continue their research individually for a time and only reconvene once more information has been gathered. Under the pretext that everyone has other duties they need to perform, and of course with the wedding just days away, there is much to be done. Then you have your week off to enjoy wedded bliss before you both readjust to your new roles and responsibilities."

"Sounds reasonable to me," agreed the King.

"I look forward to meeting Lopakka and working with Sister Fabriolla." Ahttoh put his goblet down and took a slice of cheese and wrapped it in some shaved ham before putting it onto a piece of sliced bread. Evan went to tend to the fire and Lahnni topped off everyone's drinks.

Harlonngraith reached under the table and rested his hand on Marra's leg, giving it a gentle squeeze. She brought her hand down to rest on top of his. It was nice to be with him while having a meeting. It had seemed of late that she was either talking to people about things or he was, but rarely together. And until she was confirmed as Queen she was not able to attend Council meetings with him, which took up a lot of his time.

Ahttoh finished his cheese and ham and washed it back with more cider before settling back in his seat. Marra watched his eyes flicker to her wrists, but she wore a long-sleeved blouse so her tattoos were covered.

"Would you like to see them?" she asked.

This made him jump a little and look at her guiltily. "I didn't mean to stare."

"It is fine."

"Rumor has it that your Brands are different."

"Yes," she said. But rather than explain, she rolled her sleeves up to let him see them.

"Would you mind if I touched them?"

"No, go ahead." Marra stretched her arms out across the table, wrists facing upward.

Ahttoh reached out and placed his hands over her Brands. "I settle my power, much the same way I assume the two of you do," he began to explain. "And once I do, I am shown the correct Brand for that person." The priest frowned for a moment and then stared at her. "And you did these to yourself?" He held both her arms firmly.

"Yes. It felt right."

"If you had been born here you would have been like the rest of us with two Brands. One on the wrist, the other on the hip. It's interesting how things work out. You needed the Warrior Brand to be the Champion, but now you need the Gifted Brand to fulfill whatever role the Gods have planned. If you were raised here, I wonder which Brand would have been the dominant one and shown on your wrist?" His hazel eyes lit up and he looked at her eagerly. "Would you like to see?"

"I don't think I understand what you are saying."

"I have the power to Brand you in the way the Gods intended and I am offering you that now."

Marra looked around the room. Lahnni, Evan, and Harley watched but no one told her their opinion or tried to sway her in any way. This would be completely her choice. "Just like when I got them originally done I went with my gut. This time I will do it again and say yes."

Ahttoh didn't give her the chance to change her mind. He closed his eyes and took a deep breath, his shoulders rising and his chest puffing out noticeably. A light flared under each palm, just like the symbols had on the brick arched door that activated the portal and Marra grunted in pain once. The light died down quickly and he released his hand on her left wrist to reveal the Gifted Brand, now scorched into her skin. "Interesting," he commented. "That means that your Warrior Brand should now be residing on your hip." He removed his hand from her right wrist and there was her Warrior Brand burned into her flesh—it had not disappeared.

Harley laughed, Evan chuckled, and Lahnni snorted as they took in the sight.

"Typical," her father said fondly and gave her a wink.

"Well, that was unexpected." Ahttoh looked at her family laughing in response to the unprecedented outcome.

"She needed to be a Warrior to be allowed to enter the Arena, a true Warrior, not only for that moment. She needed to meet the requirements of the Challenge. It is who she is, you can't erase that from her. It makes up her identity, and how she sees herself."

"No, that is not to what I refer," Ahttoh's eyes were wide and he looked a little rattled. He looked down at his arm and slowly turned his left wrist to reveal his Brand. The Religious symbol was gone and its place was the Gifted Brand.

"The Ternion," whispered Kahlahnni into the silence.

"I'm sorry, the what?" Ahttoh blinked as if he was clearing his mind.

Lahnni didn't answer, instead she asked another question. "Tell me, Ahttoh, are the other two who carry the Gifted symbol on their hip able to do what you did for Marra?"

"No," he said slowly. "Why?"

"Because you are now more than a priest. The Gods are revealing their hand. Can you do other things aside from put the body into stasis to allow it to heal?"

"Not that I know of."

"I think we need to bring Lopakka into this. He is the most knowledgeable in Gifts." Kahlahnni looked around the table. "He can also better explain what he thinks the Ternion is."

"Thinks?" Ahttoh asked.

"Yes, he came here in the hope of meeting you and discovering what it all means after Marra had her dream."

"You had a dream about me?" the priest asked.

Marra felt sorry for him. He was looking a little wild eyed at this point.

"Yes, we think so. I dreamed of a man in dark clothing who carried a ring of skeleton keys. He threw off his cloak to reveal the Gifted symbol glowing on his head, heart, and stomach. Lopakka believes I am the head, mother is the heart, and you are the stomach. Together the three make up something called the Ternion."

Ahttoh swallowed hard. "I see. And what do you think?"

"I think that for the first time in centuries three people in Segarris all now wear the Brand of the Gifted." Marra looked at each person in the room. Three of them were the most important people in her life. "And it terrifies me," she finished.

Chapter 19

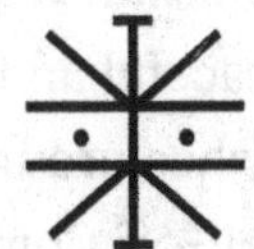

Harlonngraith

There was quiet nattering in the room as Harlonngraith waited on the dais in front of Arch Deacon Zussya, with his brother Platisse by his side as his best man. Marra had chosen her mother to be her matron of honor, which everyone but Anzhellika had thought was a marvelous idea. The former Queen had sniffed with disdain when informed, but Harlonngraith thought it was probably more to do with the fact that she had not been asked to be part of the wedding service. Even though Anzhellika had been much better at keeping her opinions to herself, and not being so critical of everything since Marra's return from the Settlement, it was still clear to everyone that she was not prepared nor willing to give up her perceived power.

Council meetings were also becoming a problem, as she interrupted people and attempted to make decisions when it was up the King. Harlonngraith had not expressly given Anzhellika a position within his council, like he had everyone else. He was at a loss at how to ask her to resign from council without hurting her feelings, for he did appreciate how much she had sacrificed for him over the years and that she had done what she thought best to keep the country safe and functioning. But Harlonngraith wanted to take Segarris in a different direction. He wanted to find a peaceful and permanent resolution to the constant skirmishes around Lobbregath, as well as improve the less well-off Commoners and Servants. He didn't want to keep it functioning, he wanted it to grow and prosper. Sadly, his mother didn't see most of the Common and Servant Branded people as anything other than dim-witted fools who had to be told how to live their lives.

Today would mark a new beginning for the monarchy of Segarris. Harlonngraith had now broken several long-standing agreements since returning from his journey to find his Champion. The Challenge for the Right to Rule had changed him in ways he was only now understanding. He had Bonded with a half Pomaikkan woman instead of marrying some noble lady from the Province of Jaggiron. Today, not only would Marra become his wife, she would also be crowned Queen. She didn't know it yet but there was a throne being installed next to his of equal grandeur and height, showing all that she was his equal in every way. This was just the beginning of ways he planned on showing her how much he loved, valued, and worshiped her. She had willingly walked into a battle to the death for him and all that he represented, and that would never be taken for granted. He now owed his title, power, and wealth to Marra, and the sooner his mother realized it, the better off they would all be. His beautiful Samarra had given up everything to be here with him.

The solo harpist strummed a pretty trill along the strings, bringing everyone's chatter to a hush. The harp had been Harlonngraith's choice, his mother had wanted a large orchestra, but Harley had felt that the single melodious instrument made the moment more intimate. There would be a full orchestra at the reception instead. As the harpist plucked the first notes of his chosen song, Harlonngraith took a moment to look out at the many affluent citizens assembled; some smiled encouragingly, some nodded as his eyes passed over them. The moment was surreal and he was going to take in as much as he could. He barely remembered the Bonding ceremony as he had been so thrilled to have Marra agree to it that it had become a whirlwind in planning to have it done before they left for the Arena. And then after the ceremony, assassins had come marring the event forever with the death of Eltta, their dear friend.

"I hope you are both ready for this," whispered Platisse.

"She was born for this," Harley replied with confidence. "Today will be perfect."

Samarra

Queen Samarra wondered just how long she had to wear the crown. It was heavy and uncomfortable, and giving her a migraine behind her right eye. The last thing Marra wanted on her wedding night was a headache interfering with her plans. She hoped that perhaps Harley would know when she could remove the crown and heavy cape that they had tied around her neck at the coronation. The sky-blue cape with its striking periwinkle blue feathered edges covered her shoulders and all but the very front of her form fitting white bridal gown. She had opted not to have a train on her dress, knowing that it would be a huge tripping hazard with the ridiculous amount of people in attendance, but the cape dragged on the floor behind her. Down the back of the cape in silver thread were embroidered all eight Brands. The cape had not been her decision but Harlonngraith's, and had caused quite a stir when she had turned to face him to receive the crown, showing the assembled guests the symbols. Marra had worn the Noble Brand on her clothing at Harlonngraith's coronation, but it was forbidden to wear the Monarch's symbol—or so she thought.

She smiled mildly at the poor joke the obviously nervous Viscount made, and hoped someone saw her plight soon and came to rescue her. Marra had very little training in court etiquette and she still wasn't sure how to get away from this type of situation. At home, a girlfriend would have saved her by now.

"Faffia, I have people I would like you to meet." Her father spoke brightly as he approached with several people in tow.

Oh, thank fuck, Marra thought to herself as she nodded her permission for the Viscount to leave. She looked at the three people standing with her father and instantly recognized they all had the same glorious aquamarine eyes. This was his family. They were her relatives. She wondered just how distant relatives they were.

Evannderth smiled warmly and came to stand beside her. "This is my father, Duke Jaronnderth Durrand." He looked at her proudly before turning to his father. "Sir, this is Queen Samarra Kahlahnni Cellecia Durrand Vissermonte, Soul Sleeper and Champion of Seggaris, and your granddaughter."

The older man, who looked to be in his mid-seventies with thinning on top gray hair, full lips and a lined forehead, like his son, bowed deeply. "That is quite the title you have there, Your Majesty."

"Yes, I can't even keep them all straight," Marra said shyly. Her heart was racing. She had never stopped to think about the fact she had family here. It had only ever been her mum and dad and her.

"This is my brother and heir to the title of Duke of Durrand, Lord Kveller." The younger brother was as tall as his sibling but had dirtier blond hair and a mischievous look on his face. He looked to be the most relaxed person in the room.

Kveller bowed as respectfully as his father had. "It is a pleasure to meet you, Your Majesty. It came as quite a surprise to discover my brother not dead but returned with the two most important women in this country. I will never know how one scruffy Warrior could get so lucky."

This made everyone laugh, and Marra found herself relaxing.

"Allow me to introduce my daughter, Lady Yesskia. She is the eldest of my children and second in line to the Durrand lands."

The pretty girl with stunning eyes and light brown hair curtsied deeply, her head lowered in respect. "Your Majesty," she said softly, her voice barely above a whisper.

Marra's heart went out to her as she recognized her own shyness in another. "Be welcome, Lady Yesskia." Samarra turned her attention back to all of them, trying not to feel overwhelmed with this influx of family. "I hope you are planning on staying for a while so we may catch up." Marra paused and looked slyly at her father. "And you can tell me all the things Dad did as a kid because he keeps trying to tell me he was perfect."

This made them all laugh, but it was cut short by the intrusion of another. "It is a pleasure to see you, Duke Durrand," Anzhellika announced as she stepped into the middle of the group, ignoring Kveller and Yesskia for the moment. Everyone bowed and curtsied.

"Tell me, has there been any push back from my son's choice to marry Samarra?" she asked pointedly.

Everyone stilled.

"Why would there be?" Jaronnderth finally responded.

"Well, Harlonngraith was supposed to marry a noble from your Province according to the treaty."

This brought a frown to the old man's face. "He did."

"I beg your pardon?" Anzhellika asked, obviously confused and a little affronted at the answer.

"He did. He married my granddaughter."

"But she doesn't carry the Noble Brand," insisted Anzhellika.

Marra stood there, amazed at how easily her mother-in-law could ignore her and carry on a conversation without giving a single indication she cared who heard. The only thing stopping Marra from running away, or worse attacking her, was the vice-like grip her father had on her arm. Marra could feel her anxiety rising as her stomach roiled with anger and embarrassment.

"Lady Anzhellika," Marra's grandfather responded with feigned surprise. The former Queen bristled at the new title. "Queen Samarra does not need the Brand of Nobility to be worthy of marrying the King, she after all, won him the throne. I defy anyone to say otherwise."

Captain Evannderth, once the Queen's most favored soldier and trusted spy, cleared his throat. "Samarra, it is time," Evan said loudly.

"It is?' Marra asked, not really sure what he meant, but going with it. Her father clearly had something in mind.

"Yes, it is time for the traditional father-daughter dance," he announced, and held out his arm to her.

"I have never heard of such a tradition," Anzhellika stated.

It seemed to Marra that Anzhellika was truly going out of her way to be difficult today. Marra squared her shoulders, screwed up her courage, swallowed her shyness in front of these recently discovered family members, and looked her new mother-in-law in the eye. "It is a new tradition. There will be many more to come now I am Queen." There was no arrogance in her voice, just quiet determination. Marra didn't wait for a response; instead, she took her father's proffered arm and walked through the crowd and onto the dance floor. "Any advice?" she asked as they began to dance.

"About what?" He laughed as he twirled her under his arm, bringing back memories of her dancing with him as a little girl.

"About how to deal with her. You worked for her for years. Quite honestly, I don't know how or why you did it."

"She is worse. Her bitterness and need for power was always there, but always covered by a veneer of gratitude and civility. I worked for King Tommofey then Anzhellika for the same reason I now work for Harlonngraith. It is my calling, my caste. I was Branded a Warrior for a reason, and I have always taken that seriously. When I started, I was only protecting a few people. Now I protect a nation, and whether they are the people I love most or perfect strangers, everyone counts," he explained.

"You are too good, Dad."

"I have my faults, like everyone else. Just ask your mum. She will be happy to list them for you."

This made them both laugh. "No, seriously... Any advice on how to handle Anzhellika?"

"Pick your battles. Let her think you are compliant and only make a stand on things that you really can't compromise on. It's what I have always done."

Marra took a moment to consider the advice. He was right. She couldn't possibly disagree with Anzhellika about everything, no matter how much she wanted to on most things. Marra needed to find a way to appease Anzhellika without compromising her own ethics, and for Harlonngraith, she would try. "Thanks, Dad. It makes a lot of sense."

"Happy to help, Faffia." He smiled at her. "Now, tell me, how many people have mentioned you starting on providing an heir yet?" he joked.

This made her grimace. "Only every second person I talk to."

The song came to an end and they both stopped and politely applauded the orchestra.

"May I have the next dance?" a deep rumbling voice asked from behind her, and Marra's insides turned gooey. His voice continued to have that effect on her and she hoped it always would.

"Of course, Your Majesty." Evan stepped back and bowed to Harlonngraith.

"Must you?" muttered Harley.

"We are in front of everyone that matters. Forms must be met," Evannderth reasoned.

"So, I shouldn't call you Dad?" Harlonngraith asked with a straight face.

This made Marra laugh, and Evan shook his head in an *oh dear* sort of way. Marra felt her heart lift. This was the man she loved, the complex King of Segarris. Harley took his role as King seriously. He was smart, educated, forward thinking, and at times a little arrogant; all good traits for a king who wanted to pave his own path, but underneath lurked a man with a wonderful sense of humor, a caring heart, an ability to forgive, and a willingness to understand others. Things few people got to witness from the King.

"Dad indeed. I wouldn't let your mother hear you say that," was Evan's comeback before he left the newly-married couple to enjoy their dance.

"Any chance I can remove this crown and cape yet?" she asked through a smile. No one needed to know how much she was coming to loathe the heaviness of both of them "Have they not been reminded enough that I am the new Queen?" The first notes of the next song began.

This made Harlonngraith laugh, as he had only been required to wear a thin coronet that sat low on his brow for the wedding and coronation. "The crown can probably come off," he admitted.

"And the cape? It is heavy and I am still unsure if it was wise to put your Brand on the back of it," she said as he drew her into his arms. Marra kept her eyes firmly on his beautiful gray ones, blocking out all the onlookers as he spun her around the now-empty dance floor. She hoped she wasn't going to trip on the too-long cape.

Harlonngraith ignored all protocol and lowered his head to kiss her cheek. "We are a team, and it was more about the symbolism that none are above you—even me."

"I don't think your brother approves much," she told him as she caught Tommofey watching them with an inscrutable stare. He looked away as soon as their eyes met.

"I am not really interested in what Platisse thinks at this moment," Harley answered, making Marra look up at him.

"I wasn't thinking about him," she said. "I was thinking about Tommofey."

"Oh, well yes. Him too. I wanted the fact that you rank above both of them, and mother for good measure, firmly in their minds before they all see the new throne I had made for you."

Marra groaned only half-jokingly. "What have you done?"

"Nothing."

"King Harlonngraith, you need to fess up."

"Or what?" he teased.

"Or my plans to tie you up and ride you like a prized stallion might have to be put aside for another time," she spoke coyly, always amazed at how he brought out this side of her. Marra didn't even blush. She had been thinking about this from the moment she had left his side to journey to the Pomaikkan city. Marra had loosely tied Harley up the first time they had slept together with her black belt, this time she would use her black belt and their Bonding ribbon. Her insides twisted with desire with the mere suggestion of tying him up.

Harley pressed her tighter against him and she could feel his growing erection, he arched an eyebrow at her. "Now, that does sound promising."

"Then spill," she ordered.

"It's nothing really. I had a throne built for you that matches mine."

"And the scandalous part?" Samarra pressed.

"I don't want to spoil the surprise." He smiled mysteriously down at her.

"If you don't tell me now, I am going to step back and show the entire court that you, Your Majesty, have a raging hard on." She smiled up at him sweetly.

He gasped in mock horror. "I have married a cruel woman."

"Harlonngraith, you cannot blindside me in these things." Her words were soft and pleading. "Anzhellika and Tommofey are wary of me already. Let's not make it worse."

He instantly looked apologetic. "You are right. I won't change what I have done but I should tell you because you might not understand the significance, but they certainly will."

"Thank you."

"I have granted you your own color, and made your throne the same height as mine, and given you your own insignia." He beamed down at her.

"You granted me a color?" she asked, confused. "What the hell does that mean?"

"My color is a pale sky-blue," he began and Marra nodded. "Tommofey's is a navy, and Platisse, though he no longer associates with it, was a mid-tone sky-blue."

"Okay, but what has that got to do with me?"

"I want you to be clear that I see you as your own person, not an extension of me and my crown, and I want others to do the same. So, I assigned you a color and insignia."

"What color?" She was now curious.

"Periwinkle." Harley beamed at her. "The color embroidered into our Bonding ribbon."

"And the insignia?"

"Why a periwinkle blue feather, of course. It is embroidered onto the back padded area of your throne.
Your father told me that the feather always represented
freedom for your mother, I thought it fitting for you too."

"Oh, Harley, that is perfect and thoughtful, and can you
actually do that?"

He rolled his glorious eyes at her and lowered his head
to her ear where his voice rumbled and her panties became instantly saturated. "I can do whatever the hell I
want. I will never stop showing you how grateful I am for
all you have sacrificed for me."

"But you were also willing to give it all up for me and
live a humble life teaching middle-aged women and children self-defense." Her gut roiled at the memory of those
middle-aged women touching Harley and the fight they
had had after because she was jealous.

"Ha! Grown-ups and kids, fine; but I would have made
you do that midday self-defense class." He kissed her
cheek on the way back to standing fully straight, and
Marra just stopped herself from grinning at the collective
sigh of women enjoying the romantic gesture.

"I love you." Marra fought the urge to move her hand
and wrap her fist in his hair.

"I love you more."

"And can I just say that your party planning skills are on
point and all future royal events will be planned by you?
This wedding is wonderful, thank you."

Harley bent down and kissed the tip of her nose and the court ladies audibly swooned. "Maybe the next one we plan together."

"Mind if we join you?" asked Kahlahnni as Evan twirled her next to them before settling his hand on the small of her back. Anzhellika and Platisse joined them too, and as Marra walked around Harley as the dance dictated, she caught the eye of Tommofey and her heart broke for him. For a mere moment, she saw the pain and grief he hid from everyone, and she knew in some ways she was the cause of it. The prince's face changed to its familiar haughty, ever so slightly annoyed handsome mask, and he glared at her before turning to engage in conversation with the man standing next to him.

Harley spun Marra a little faster than he should, and she felt her heavy crown slip. This brought her attention back to where it should be. "Protocol or not, it's definitely time to get this thing off," she announced to the small group.

"You have to cut the cake first," Anzhellika told her.

For a split second, Marra thought about arguing with her, but she remembered her father's words. *Pick your battles.* "No problem. Let's get this cake cut then."

"That's my girl," laughed Harley as they stopped dancing, and he took her arm.

"Just one thing," Marra said under her breath as they walked toward the seven-layered sugar spun monstrosity. "You even think about shoving a piece of cake in my face, I will break every bone in your hand."

Harley looked alarmed. "Why would I do that?" he asked. "It could ruin your dress or your make-up or hair. You took so much time to look beautiful today, why would I humiliate you like that in front of everyone? I also do not want you breaking my hand." He added with a wink.

And at that moment, any doubt that had been lurking in the very back of Marra's mind floated away. This man was her world.

Chapter 20

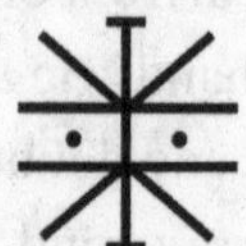

Harlonngraith

The final lace-covered button came undone, and he watched with wicked delight as the pure white wedding dress slid over the perfect silhouette of Samarra's long lean body and defined legs in the soft firelight. The King of Segarris lay naked and spread eagled upon the blankets of his huge bed. His torso was propped up to a semi-sitting position by several fluffy pillows and his cock lay hard and twitchy against his stomach. He pulled against the restraints that held him in place, for not the first time, and was still a little surprised that he had allowed himself to be this vulnerable to another human. Even though the human was his Bonded and now wife, it was still difficult to be completely at someone's mercy by choice when he was raised to be in control of everything at all times.

Harley watched Samarra glide toward him and caught his bottom lip in his teeth, and again strained against the bonds of the black belt and Bonding ribbon, hoping to break free and reach out and caress her soft, supple skin. But the damn ties held him in place. It was intoxicating and frustrating in equal parts. He growled and her response was a throaty laugh.

She slowly knelt on the bed and crawled up between his thighs, her hands coming to rest on either side of his head. Marra bent down and gently ran her nose along his, her breath hot on his face. She brushed her lips across his, barely touching him and Harley had just enough leverage on his ties to push up and kiss her fully. The kiss was slow, hot, and languid. He moaned softly, uncontrollably.

Marra broke the kiss and pushed herself up, bringing her hands slowly down his chest, tweaking each nipple as she did so. She settled back onto her feet, still kneeling between his legs. Without breaking eye contact, she lifted her palm to her mouth and licked it several times, it was one of the hottest things Harley had ever witnessed. Marra took his cock into her now wet hand and ran her thumb over the top before squeezing him gently. He bucked under her but continued to hold her gaze.

With one hand pumping him, she put the fingers of her other hand into her mouth and wet them before trailing them down her sternum and circling them around her nipples.

"Fuck." the word rumbled out of him as he threw his head back and pulled harder against the restraints.

He felt Marra move her legs, while not letting go of him. Harley raised his head and watched as she straddled him, but with her back to him. With her hand that still slowly moved up and down, she guided him to her entrance, and inch by inch lowered herself on him. Marra rolled her hips and the heat in his center exploded. If she kept that up, he wouldn't be able to stop himself from coming.

"If you don't untie me now, I am going to..." he threatened, but his voice trailed off. What was he really going to do?

"Oh, my King, what will you do?" she crooned, calling his bluff. "Yell for one of your servants? Do you want to be caught like this?" Marra asked as she continued to slowly slide up and down his cock.

"Marra, please," he begged as he pulled against the restraints. The last time she had tied him they had been loose enough that if he wanted to he could have got out of them, and he had not been tethered to anything. His heels dug into the bed and his hips involuntarily rose to meet her.

"No," she answered. Marra leaned forward and placed her hands on his thighs digging her nails in. "I want you to submit, let your mind go, and just feel. Let everything go." She began to rock her hips higher and come down harder and faster, her gorgeous ass now slapping his stomach.

Harley pushed his head back deeper into the pillows and bit his lip as his breathing became ragged and his eyes lost focus. He tasted blood and he didn't care. He braced himself as she rode him. He was so close. "Stop, Samarra. If you love me, you will stop," he begged, but not a teasing sensual way, this was a heartfelt plea.

She stilled immediately. Harley held on, his heart was racing, and his cock wanted to know what the fuck he was doing. But his head won. "I want to see you, not your back. I want to see your face," he tried to explain.

"Damn you and your romance, King Harlonngraith." She spoke quietly and he couldn't tell if she was angry or disappointed. She leaned forward, and deftly untied the knots on the silk scarves that held his ankles in place. With admirable expertise, they didn't lose contact as she swung her legs and body around so she was still strad-dling him but facing him. Marra kissed the tip of his nose and then untied his hands.

He didn't wait for her permission, he lifted her off him for a moment and held her close as he picked her up enough to swing his legs underneath him then moved to lay her down on her back. Her legs were now wrapped around his waist. Harley entered her as he lay flat against her chest, covering as much of her as he could with his bigger body.

"You are my everything," he whispered as he lowered his lips to hers. "I hope you never regret it." He finally voiced the fear that had been growing louder in his head the past few weeks.

Marra brought her hands to his face and cupped his cheeks gently, running her thumbs along his cheekbones. He continued to rock against her, pushing up in a rolling motion rather than in and out. The feeling was sublime. Harley leaned his forehead on hers and they watched each other, their breathing loud and heavy.

"You are beautiful," she breathed, her voice hitching at the end, giving him the indication that she was as close as he was to climaxing. "And mine," she murmured as she stilled under him for several moments before she began to shudder. Her core tensed and released as Marra rode her orgasm, pulling Harley along and helping him fall into his own vortex of pleasure.

Chapter 21

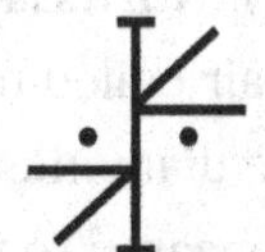

Tommofey

The sleek fast boat, rowed by ten brawny men, flew across the wide river that wound its way through the Twin Cities of Segarris. The gentle rocking of the boat made Tom slightly queasy. He had possibly drunk a little too much red wine at the reception. He stood looking out over the inky black water and hoped he wouldn't embarrass himself by having to throw up over the side. The wind whipped his brown hair back from his face and he took in large steadying gulps of air. He was a prince of the realm, he refused to vomit.

It had been an interesting night that made Tommofey acutely aware that his continued acceptance into society hinged upon the open support of his brother, Harlonngraith, and his new wife. He had spent a vast amount of time watching Queen Samarra from a distance. His feelings for her continued to alternate between rage at her being the reason he was not King and married to Aviva, and finding the tall warrior woman fascinating. She was beautiful in her white, floor-length bridal gown with its tight-fitting lace overlay encrusted with sparkling diamonds in an intricate pattern that wound from her shoulder across the bodice, around her back and ended on her lower hip. The dress was stunning in its simplicity, even though it was fussy with its lace and diamonds. With her long dark blonde hair coiled up in rolls on her head, interspersed with more diamonds, and moderately high satin shoes, Samarra appeared to be almost as tall as her husband. They made an impressive couple.

Tommofey had found himself daydreaming about Aviva and what type of wedding dress she would have worn. It had come with a sad moment of realization that he hadn't spent enough time with her to learn those little things, and the only person that might know was also gone. The bride had snatched that away from him. And on that sour note, he had decided it was time to go home.

As Tom had begun to say his goodbyes, he had been approached by Captain Evannderth.

"A word before you leave?" the older man had asked.

"Of course."

Evannderth led the Prince to a quieter part of the room where no one could possibly overhear them. "I have been informed that you have been told about my daughter's dream regarding your mother?"

"Yes, though I am not sure how much credit I should give it."

Captain Evannderth had raised an eyebrow at him. "I hope you have spoken to Captain Albertinne about our concerns and he has added more security?"

Tommofey had straightened his shoulders at that point, and looked down on the middle-aged man, who had served his father but had spied on his mother. There were still so many underlying feelings towards this family. "Yes. Though I would encourage you to watch your own and I will take care of mine." Tom knew he had been a tad rude, but the memory of the King and Queen dancing happily and being joined by their family had stung, and Samarra catching him feeling that way had made him feel vulnerable.

"Of course, Your Highness." Evannderth had nodded politely. "I meant no implication that your soldiers were not up to the task, I merely wanted to make certain you understood that we take Marra's dreams seriously."

Tommofey pushed the conversation aside as a gust of wind made him stumble slightly, and he grasped the rail of the boat tighter. He thought about what Evannderth had said, that they took Samarra's dreams seriously. Tom had to admit he found it strange to rely on a Seer and Soul Sleeper who could potentially make up anything they wanted to get people to comply. He had never spoken to Samarra or Kahlahnni about their special abilities—somewhere in the back of his mind he wondered why. There must be something holding him back from finding out more. Or could it be that if he talked to them about it, he might feel obliged to agree to a reading and he couldn't control that outcome?

The private dock of the royal family came into view and Tom furrowed his brow when he took in the amount of torches that awaited him. Why was there a crowd on the dock? It was well past midnight. He had only left a small troop of men at the dock with his carriage. Ten at the dock and ten accompanied him to the royal wedding. As they sped closer, it appeared that a full squad of fifty men stood waiting.

Tom's heart pounded and sound rushed in his ears as he tried to shun the random thought that something had happened while he had been gone. It didn't take them much longer to reach their assigned port and come alongside the dock. And waiting for him was both Albertinne and Prynnan. "What has happened?" he demanded as soon as he was close enough to not yell.

"Your Highness, this way to the carriage," Albertinne held out his hand. "Please," he added, which was the only thing that stopped Tom from screaming at him to just bloody well tell him.

He was escorted quickly to the carriage and installed in there, Griggory being told that he could ride up front with the driver rather than sit with the prince. "Prince Tommofey," Albertinne began. "There is no easy way to say this. Your mother was murdered approximately a turning and a half ago. I am deeply sorry for your loss. We will get you home safely and quickly." And without further words, the Warrior who would no doubt be feeling the responsibility of having this happen on his command, closed the door and told the driver to move out.

Something settled into the pit of Tom's stomach and curled around his spine. The nausea he had felt on the boat trip doubled and his mouth had grown dry. He counted to three, breathed in, and then three again, and released the breath. He willed himself not to cry. Instead, he turned his thoughts to those who would want this the most.

His mother was killed by suspected assassins, and to Tom, that pointed to the same person or people who had sent the ones when he was on his way to the Arena. It could be Harlonngraith, or now he had met her a few times, it was a definite possibility it was Anzhellika. Either way, they will pay for this. That woman had no qualms about showing how much she detested her nephew. It was very convenient that tonight Evannderth had sought him out to make certain he had taken heed of the warning of Samarra's dream. Tom didn't know which one of the two he suspected had done this, but one of them would pay. A slow painful death, and then he would take the crown and rule as his mother had always wanted him to.

Tommofey's anger boiled over and he swore viciously before lashing out and pummelling the soft cushion on the opposite seat. Tears ran down his face as the sudden realization that he was truly alone in this world sunk in. He had no one.

Chapter 22

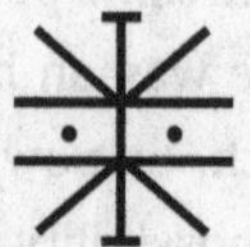

Harlonngraith

Dawn was approaching and they were only now going to sleep. Harlonngraith and Samarra had spent their wedding night making love and enjoying each other's company. Neither spoke of their Bonding night and the assassins attack, rather they reveled in each other's company and spoke quietly of the life they hoped to have together. Harley had been right; it had been a perfect day.

The King was the most relaxed he had been in months, possibly since he had begun looking for his Champion. He snuggled deeper into his bed sheets and pulled Marra closer, gently humming and hoping that it would put her to sleep. He didn't mind doing it even though he got less sleep. He loved her and was secretly relieved that she had agreed to marry him. He would sing her to sleep every night for the rest of his life if that would bring her peace and happiness.

At the moment, Marra was having a difficult time adjusting to her new life and he knew it, and he helplessly didn't know what to do about it. Harlonngraith was so busy all day, every day, making little decisions and big decisions—he had had no concept of how much work it was to rule the kingdom properly. Anybody could be king, but to be a good king took work. Lots and lots of hard, dedicated, self-sacrificing work. He knew he had to find a way to work smarter and not harder, and he had to find people he trusted to run things for him, but all of that would take time. And until that happened, he was just going to have to take on more than necessary and hope that Marra understood—but tonight was about them.

Everything he had planned to make their day special had gone without a hitch. His mother had been instrumental in making certain he didn't forget any minor details, but when Harley had realized that it was becoming more about her and how she pictured it, he had given her the job of being in charge of the food and beverages and had taken over all other planning.

BANG. BANG. BANG.

Someone pounded on the door, giving them both a fright and making Marra instantly reach under her pillow and pull out one of the blue bladed daggers she had thrown at him all those months ago. Harley tried to hide his shock, but muttered at her as he climbed out of bed to throw on a robe, "We will speak about bringing knives to bed later. I could have cut my hand sliding it under your pillow," he pointed out.

Marra looked guilty for a moment. "Yeah, sorry, didn't think of that." She climbed out of bed and reached under the mattress and pulled out the second matching dagger and handed it to him. "Just in case," Marra said as she threw on his crumpled shirt she had retrieved from the floor.

BANG. BANG. BANG.

"Yes?" called Harlonngraith as Marra moved to stand in front of him. He was not stupid enough to tell her that he could take care of himself.

The door swung open and a distressed looking guard, that Harlonngraith instantly recognizes as one of his mother's personal bodyguards, was standing there. He had a large head gash and held on to an hysterically sobbing young lady-in-waiting, whose night dress was covered in blood.

"What has happened?" he demanded.

"Your Majesty, someone has attacked your mother."

"Let's go," ordered Marra, who didn't look back at him. She headed straight for the door.

It felt like forever to get to the suites of his mother, but it was only two hallways down in actuality. As his own personal guards gathered around him, Harley wanted to push them away. He felt claustrophobic, hemmed in, and he wanted to scream that there had been a mistake. His thoughts were racing. "Can anyone tell me what happened?" He looked to the guard who was leading the way, still holding tightly to the now quietly sobbing lady-in-waiting. "What happened to your head?"

"Larrs and I were on duty, Your Majesty. The door opened and I turned, thinking it was either Yalenna or your mother. Instead, it was someone dressed in black." The soldier was stumbling over his words, rushing to get them out. "Larrs was already crumpling to the ground from a knife to the throat before we had time to react. I went to grab him rather than get my sword out and he slashed at me. I fell backward, making a hell of a racket."

"Probably saved your life," remarked Marra as they turned down the final corridor.

"How so?"

"If you had gone for your sword rather than rush at them they would have had time to place their knife thrust better. By instantly reacting and stepping forward, you gave them less space to kill you. The noise of you falling and your sword clattering would have brought a guard stationed at the end of the corridor, so he had to go," Marra explained.

Harlonngraith had half listened as they continued to hurry and had to admit it made sense. They arrived at the door to find it open. Without stopping, Harley rushed into the huge private parlor and through to his mother's bedroom to find her lying on her bed, her blue eyes wide open in terror. Anzhellika was taking quick shallow breaths and holding her stomach. Blood seeped through her fingers and quickly pooled onto the bedspread.

"Get my mother and father and send to the Order of Segarris for Brother Atthol to be brought here immediately." Samarra took control. "Get me a towel, we need to apply pressure."

Harlonngraith was relieved and grateful for Marra stepping up as his thoughts were hectic as he settled on the bed next to his mother. He picked up one of her sticky, bloody hands and brought it to his chest. "Hang on, we are getting help," he told her.

Marra knelt on the other side of the bed and gently removed Anzhellika's hand, revealing a thick slash under her rib cage. She pressed the towel firmly over the bleeding wound.

"I am sorry," Harley whispered, his voice nearing breaking point. "I tried to protect you. I thought I had done enough." *This can't be happening*, his brain kept repeating. "Keep fighting, you need to be here to see your grandchildren, to see what you fought for to continue."

Anzhellika continued to look up, her eyes blinking slowly. She attempted to speak, but only a gurgling sound came out. She began to cough and blood sprayed over Harley as he leaned over her.

Yalenna, the young lady-in-waiting, screamed hysterically and Marra again took control. "Get her out of here, take her into the parlor," she ordered. "Get her a drink but keep her in sight. We don't know what's happened yet, or if she's involved."

Harley looked over his shoulder at the sound of rushing feet. Evannderth and Kahlahnni hurried into the room and both stopped. They had arrived quicker than what he thought they would as the Seer chose to sleep in a less crowded section of the palace. "I sensed something was wrong," she announced.

"They were already awake and dressed when we got there," the guard announced unnecessarily.

Harley turned back to his mother whose breathing had become more ragged, her chest rattled, and her eyes were now closed. "Faffia, you can let go now. Harley needs you," the King heard Evannderth say, though he didn't bother to see what was happening. He felt the movement of the bed and a few moments later, Marra stood behind him, her hand on his shoulder.

"Harlonngraith, look at me," Lahnni said softly.

He did what he was told, slowly turning his head to find the Seer now sitting on the other side of his mother, Evannderth behind her, but his hands were now holding the bloodstained towel in place.

"I want to read your mother. I want to see if her mind can give me any clue at what happened here tonight. Are you understanding me?"

Harley frowned as he thought about the words. "Can you not wait until she gets better?"

"Harley..." It was Marra. "Can you afford to not know what she saw if she doesn't get better?"

He didn't want to consider it. The idea of his mother dying was too much. But he was King, and these decisions were his to make. He remembered Evannderth reminding him to think straight and grieve later when Marra had been dying. "Yes, I give you permission."

Kahlahnni didn't wait. She reached out and placed her hand on the cheek of Anzhellika. Harley watched and waited. His mother's breathing stopping and starting, like she was holding her breath and then fighting to inhale. She struggled one final time and her chest stopped moving. There was no more noise, the room was silent. Too silent.

"Rest, Anzhellika," Lahnni said gently as she removed her hand from the former queen's face.

"What did you see?" whispered Harley, his voice breaking as he mutely willed his mother's chest to rise and fall, but it stubbornly stayed still.

"Betrayal."

This story continues in
Denial
Book 5
Right to Rule Series
Who is behind the assassinations and what is their end game?

The death of his mother is the final straw and Prince Tommofey is now out for revenge. All things point to his brother, King Harlonngraith, but Tom is conflicted. The more time he spends in the King and Queen's company the less he hates them. Is he in denial of the truth or is there more to uncover behind what seems like the ultimate betrayal?

Queen Samarra, Soul Sleeper of Segarris, feels guilty. Could she have done more to prevent the death of her family members? She is beginning to feel that she has made a serious error in coming to this land and believing she could make a difference. If only her dreams could reveal her future.

King Harlonngraith is desperate. When he won the crown he believed things were supposed to get better, not worse. He is mourning the loss of his mother and no one can tell him why the assassins were sent. He is determined to uncover the traitor who let the assassins in, but where does he begin?

Excerpt from Denial

"I am doing everything in my power to help you. I know what you experienced was life changing, but you won't let me in to help you."

"Are you really trying to help me?" she asked, thumping her fist on the table as she stood. Her control over her temper fraying. "Or are you trying to ease your own guilt?"

"My guilt?" he shouted, as he also surged to his feet. "What do you mean by that?"

"For fuck sake, Harley. All of us carry guilt and all of us have to reconcile ourselves to it. We have all made choices and in the end that has cost people's lives, whether it be by our own hand or another's. You tried to appease your guilt by forgiving your brother, but you need to forgive yourself. Instead you bury yourself in work and avoid me."

"That's what you think? That I am avoiding you?" Harlonngraith asked evenly.

"I don't know what to think. I know that you have many things to decide and there is so much at stake that I didn't want to add to it." She was becoming exasperated.

"So you went to Tom instead of me for comfort and support?" He was clearly hurt. "Is he there for you in any other ways?"

"You're an asshole."

Warrior Brand

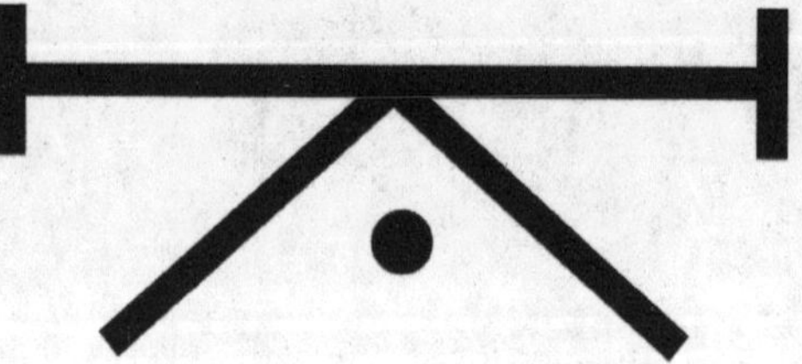

Religious Brand

Servant Brand

Commoner Brand

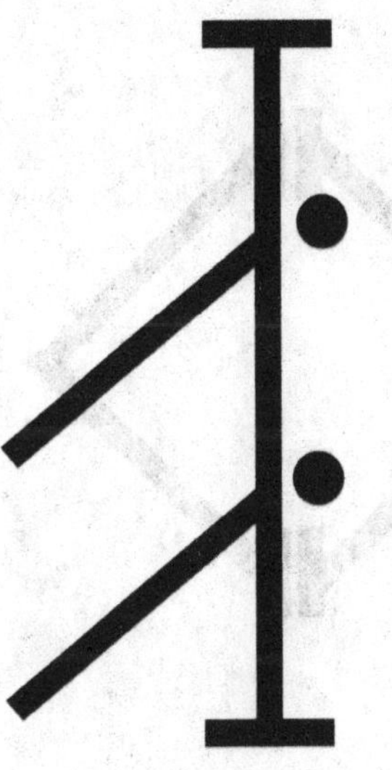

Roamer Brand

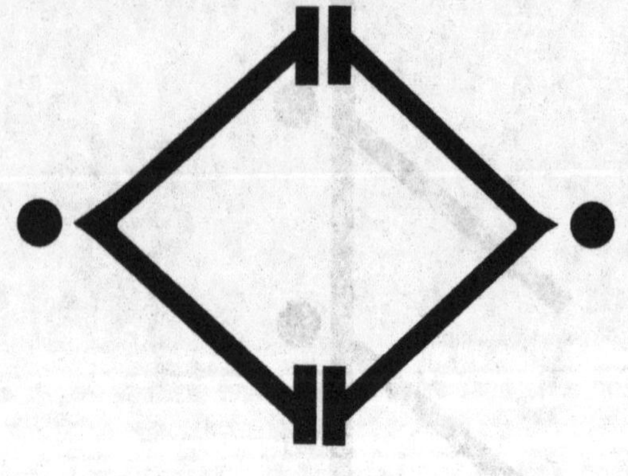

Gifted Brand

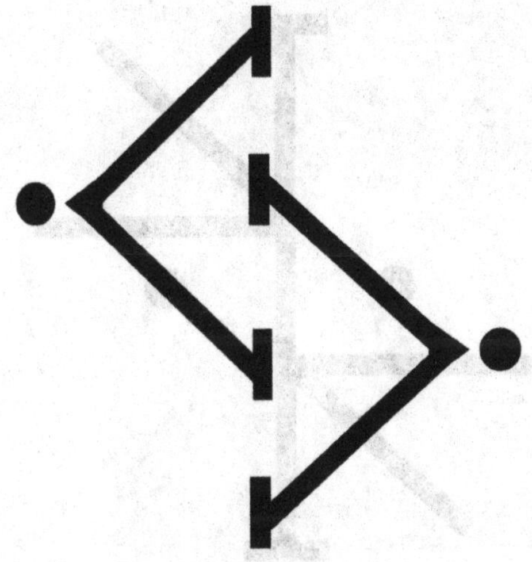

Noble Brand

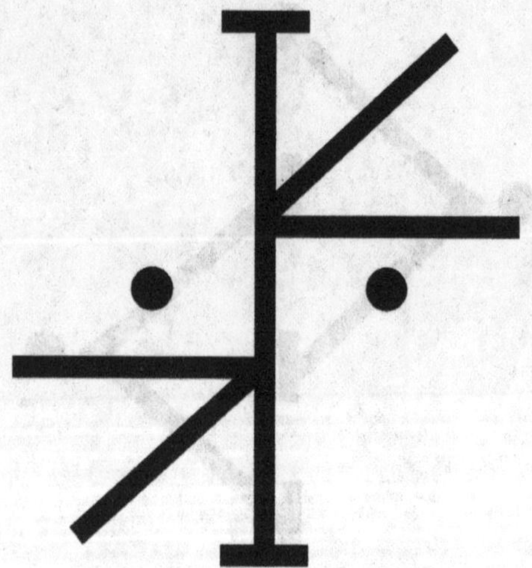

Monarch Brand

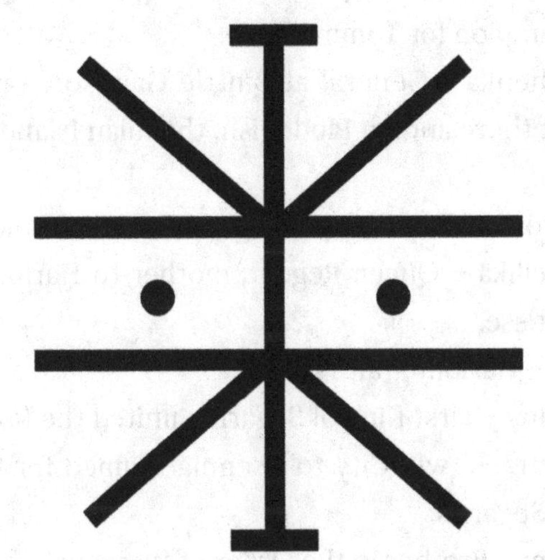

Glossary

Aislynn – Lady of Burrop.

Albertinne (Captain) - Leading the group finding the Champion for Tommofey.

Alloshenka - General at Binttle Garrison - runs the outpost there and on Pluddgish, the mian Island of Lobbregath.

Ambrosse – Boy in orphanage in Gennestenmont.

Anzhellika – Queen Regent, mother to Harlonngraith and Platisse.

Arris – Harlonngraith's Page.

Arsenny – First King of Segarris, united the Provinces.

Arsenny – Twin City to Csennia. Named for the first king of Segarris.

Arttem – Brother in the Order of Wasshu.

Aviva - Servant, Shai's sister.

Binttle - Town in the North East of Segarris in the Province of Jaggiron. Overlooks the Islands of Lobbregath.

Cellecia – Guardian of Kahlahnni. Wife of Emmettin. Mother of Margueritte, Mechelle, and Mattilde.

Channing – Lord of Burrop.

Correntin – Sergeant in Segarrin army.

Csennia – Twin city to Arsenny. Named for the first queen of Segarris.

Daiisi - General Alloshenka's horse.

Dancing Boar - name of an Inn.

Darria – Once Queen, now Lady. Mother to Tommofey.

Darvell - Stablemaster in the garrison of Binttle.

Ellei – Pomaikkan woman.

Eltta – Pomaikkan instructor.

Emmettin Finnley – Former Captain in Segarrin navy. Husband to Cellecia, father of Margueritte, Mechelle, and Mattilde. Guardian of Kahlahnni.

Evannderth Durrand – Sergeant, then Captain in the army of Segarris. Bonded to Kahlahnni, father of Samarra.

Fabriolla – Sister in the Order of Seggar.

Fabbron - Drill Sergeant in Brinttle.

Fennkston - Mayor of Binttle.

Gallya – Samarra's maid.

Griggory - Tommofey's Page.

Harlonngraith – First born son to King Tommofey and Queen Anzhellika.

Heiranni – Pomaikkan instructor for the Gifted. Father to Lopakka.

Innessa – Sister of the Order of Seggar.

Ittaie – General in Segarris army.

Jaronnderth Durrand (Duke) – Evannderth's father.

Jossiner – Laundry owner in Gennestenmont.

Kahlahnni – Seer of Segarris.

Kveller Durrand (Lord) – Evannderth's younger brother.

Larrs – Anzhellika's personal guard.

Laurynnse - Groomsman for Prince Tommofey.

Lavee – Brother in the Order of Seggar.

Lopakka – Pomaikkan instructor for the Gifted. Son of Heiranni.

Lyubbov - one of the Servants at Binttle. Roommate of Aviva.

Malekko – Pomaikkan instructor.

Marggot – Worked in laundry in Gennestenmont.

Margueritte – Eldest child of Cellecia and Emmettin. Sister of Mechelle and Mattilde.

Mattilde – Third born child of Cellecia and Emmettin. Sister of Margueritte and Mechelle.

Mechelle – Second child of Cellecia and Emmettin. Sister of Margueritte and Mattilde.

Nikkitta - one of the Servants at Binttle. Roommate of Aviva.

Ottilie - Housekeeper in charge of Binttle garrison.

Pattraic – Harlonngraith's servant.

Peggy – Evannderth's maid in the palace.

Pepper - Aviva's horse.

Platisse – Second born son to King Tommofey and Queen Anzhellika. Brother of Harlonngraith and Tommofey.

Pynnan - Warrior escorting Prince Tommofey.

Ripperedst - Village in Wasshun Province.

Ruby – Kahlahnni's Horse.

Russlongraith – King of Seggaris. Changed the Branding Ceremony.

Samarra – Daughter of Kahlahnni and Evannderth. Soul Sleeper of Segarris. Champion to Prince Harlongraith.

Shacram - Disc like weapon attached to a chain. Common to the Islands of Lobbregath.

Shai - Tommofey's Champion. Aviva's brother.

Shullamith – Priest of the Order of Seggar.

Sittiq – Brother in the Order of Seggar.

Toby - Tommofey's horse.

Tommofey 2nd – Former King of Segarris.

Tommofey 3rd - Prince of Segarris. Mother - Lady Darris, father - King Tommofey, half brother to Harlonngraith and Platisse.

Tommofey – Third born son to King Tommofey, first born to Lady Darria. Half-brother to Harlonngraith and Platisse.

Traiss – Inn Keeper's daughter in Gennestenmont.

Yalenna – Anzhellika's Lady-in-waiting.

Yesskia Durrand (Lady) – Daughter of Kveller, niece to Evannderth. Cousin to Samarra.

Zussya – Arch Deacon of the Order of Seggar.

About Taya Rune

Taya Rune is a writer of romance, a sucker for happy endings, and has a knack for asking people uncomfortable questions.

She is a USA Today Bestselling Author and a finalist for the 2022 Romantic Book of the Year, for the Romance Writer's of Australia RuBY awards. Taya has had her work published in many different anthologies and publications.

Romantic Women's Fiction

Reflections of Love Collection

Also releasing on Radish and available in Audio format

Hannah

Samantha

Olivia

Chloe

Lacy

Grace

Reflections of Love Novella Collection Volume 1

(Contains books 1 – 4)

For more information on all titles head to tayarune.com

Acknowledgments

I would like to take a few moments
to say thank you.

To my children, thank you for
teaching me to let go of the small stuff. I am proud of you.

To my family, thank you for the
love and support you have shown me throughout the
years.

To my friends, the ones that have
my back and are forever in my corner – I cherish you.

To my editor, Rochelle J. Simas – IDK art.
Thank you for the kind words that
always accompany the return of my fabulously edited
manuscripts.

To my ARC, Street, Beta, and Proofreader Teams.
You are appreciated.

Follow her on your favorite
platform:

Website:
https://www.tayarune.com

Facebook:
https://www.facebook.com/taya.rune.75

Facebook Group:
https://www.facebook.com/groups/tayasromanticreal
m

Instagram:
https://www.instagram.com/tayarune/

Bookbub:
https://www.bookbub.com/authors/taya-rune

Goodreads:
https://www.goodreads.com/author/show/21156065.T
aya_Rune

Pinterest:
https://www.pinterest.com.au/TayaRune

Taya Rune

www.ingramcontent.com/pod-product-compliance
Lightning Source LLC
Chambersburg PA
CBHW010540170726
48285CB00008B/2699